ABOUT THE

George G. Gilman ... ... a
small village east of London. He attended local schools
until the age of fifteen. Upon leaving school he
abandoned all earlier ambitions and decided to become
a professional writer, with strong leanings towards the
mystery novel. He wrote short stories and books during
evenings, lunch hours, at weekends, and on the time of
various employers while he worked for an international
newsagency, a film company, a weekly book-trade
magazine and the Royal Air Force.

His first short (love) story was published when he was
sixteen and the first (mystery) novel ten years later. He
has been a full-time writer since 1970, writing mostly
Westerns which have been translated into a dozen
languages and have sold in excess of 16 million copies.
He is married and lives on the Dorset coast, which is as
far west as he intends to move right now.

THE SUNSET RIDE

George G. Gilman

NEW ENGLISH LIBRARY

for:
JOHN DRIVER
who has read as
many as anybody.

A New English Library Original Publication, 1986

First NEL Paperback Edition April 1986

NEL Books are published by
New English Library,
Mill Road, Dunton Green,
Sevenoaks, Kent.
Editorial office: 47 Bedford Square, London WC1B 3DP

Typeset by Hewer Text Composition Services, Edinburgh

Printed and bound by Hunt Barnard Printing Ltd, Aylesbury, Bucks

British Library C.I.P.
Gilman, George G.
 The sunset ride.—(Adam Steele; 40)
 Rn: Terry Harknett   I. Title   II. Series
 823'.914[F]   PR6058.A686/

ISBN 0 450 05905 7

1

The woman, who was badly hurt, had dragged herself more than sixty feet in an unsuccessful attempt to get to the baby, which was sleeping. This was clear to read in the sign: the dust disturbed and stained darkly at irregular intervals between the patch of ground where she had first begun to lose blood and the point where the strength had deserted her, when her outstretched hands were some dozen or so feet short of touching the infant.

Both were black: the colour of the woman's skin starkly contrasted on the near white of the dusty ground beneath her prone, naked form; while the baby was swathed in a white shawl and wore a blue-ribbon-trimmed white bonnet so that just the ebony-hued face was visible.

Adam Steele, who was not overly familiar with children of any age, guessed the baby was not yet six months old. He had a little more experience of women—fully clothed and otherwise—and even before he saw her face he knew for certain that this one was young: maybe was no more than a girl. Violence was not strange to him at all: and thus did he ensure that this latest incursion of other people's suffering into his life posed no immediate threat to his well-being before he paid more than cursory attention to the figures on the ground.

He had almost satisfied himself of this before he reined in the two-horse team and brought the wagon to a halt: far enough away from the woman and baby so that the dust raised by the wheels and hooves did not drift and settle on them. Then, in the moments of silence, he listened intently. And his ears confirmed what his eyes and his sixth sense for latent danger had already signalled—nobody was waiting and watching from hiding with a hostile intent toward him.

Then he applied the brakes and wound the reins around the lever. And took a worse-for-wear sheepskin coat from among the varied freight in the back of the open wagon before he climbed down from the high seat and moved forward to take a closer look at the cause of his unscheduled stop.

First, he dropped to his haunches beside the baby, and without touching the infant made sure that his initial impression had been correct. And he vented a non-committal grunt when he saw that the baby boy was unhurt and simply serenely asleep. Next he turned his attention to the woman: already aware that she was little more than twenty years old and that she was unlikely to live very much longer. For he could see her young face in profile, its expression of despair not relieved by unconsciousness; and had been able to hear her laboured breathing ever since he halted the wagon. This raggedness of the sucking in and exhalation of breath, along with the amount of blood she had lost, had to indicate that her life had almost run its course.

Gently, Steele eased the doomed young woman over on to her back. And eyed the awesome wound in her lower belly with the same brand of cold impassivity as he had glanced at her nude slenderness: before he arranged her arms at her sides and draped the coat over her. She was no taller than five feet, and the sheepskin reached from her neck to her knees. A groan, more of hopelessness than pain, had sounded from deep in her throat as he rolled her cautiously on to her back. Then she uttered another sound, something like a forlorn sigh, as he raised her head and lowered it onto a pillow fashioned from his folded-up suit jacket. But there was not even the slightest flicker of eyelashes to suggest she was on the brink of returning to consciousness.

They had cut her sex out of the black woman: sliced deep into the pit of her belly and crotch to carve out a wedge of living tissue.

That there had been more than one sadistic attacker of the woman Steele saw from the sign in the dust close to the large patch of dried blood which marked where the obscene mutilation of her body was inflicted. Three of them, he was sure. One had smoked a cigar to a small stub. Somebody chewed tobacco. The tracks of a trio of horses seemed to confirm his estimate of the number of men from their footprints. Which meant the woman had not gotten here on a horse—unless riding double with one of the men. When they had left here, the men had taken everything they came with, except for the cigar butt and some brown-stained saliva. Everything, too, that the woman had brought here: except for the baby boy and whatever was left of her life.

Here was a strip of fringe land between the northern edge of the Mojave Desert and the southern foothills of the Sierra Nevada range in central California. It was not on a trail, for Steele had elected to swing to the west when the marked trail he had followed northward for so many miles had run off the desert floor. He had steered the wagon into the turn and started to head across what he hoped was uninhabited terrain more than two hours earlier, when it was a little before midday and the low sky was threatening rain. But the weather had brightened and there had been nothing to indicate that any other human presence had ever before intruded into this piece of country: until he reached the end of a low escarpment and had to swing to the south to pass between the rock face

7

and a stand of pines that was just as much of an obstacle to the big hay wagon he was driving.

It was as he completed the turn that he saw the figures on the ground at a distance of three hundred feet or so: the infant peacefully sleeping on an area of lush green grass at the base of one of the towering pines, while the woman, mercifully unconscious, was sprawled at the side of the broad strip of rock-hard ground that extended from the base of the escarpment's end to the timber.

Now, having seen the scant sign that marked where the trio of men had brutalised the woman, and taken note that they had reached here from the south and ridden off back in the same direction, Steele spared a few more silent moments to look beyond the immediate vicinity and to listen for sounds that were not bird calls: the scurrying of land-bound creatures through the brush under the trees, and the rustling of foliage moved by a new, gentle breeze. Then he made a small sound of self-disgust and returned to the wagon. Had to climb up onto a front wheel hub to reach into the rear and bring out a canteen. Took a mouthful of water and spat it out. Immediately was unable to recall the taste of the particular brand of apprehension that he had experienced even after he was sure no one was looking down at him from the top of the escarpment or watching him from within the timber. Which he should have figured out from the dryness of the black woman's blood and the age of the cigar butt and tobacco juice, without recourse to instinct.

But, he excused himself without too much conviction as he moved toward the woman who was going to die soon, he considered he had never been this close to fulfilling his dream before. And no one had better cause than him to be concerned by any side issue, no matter what form it took, that demanded his attention along the trail to the realisation of that ambition. Too often before he had lost far more than mere time when events beyond his control,

8

and often none of his business, had distracted him. And he had found his life was on the line for something less pressing than a healthy young baby and a mutilated woman at death's door.

'Zachery?'

She spoke the name in a faint whisper while her eyes remained closed. And the intonation of her rasping voice made the single word a rhetorical question that she was sure would be answered in a manner that made hope futile.

'If that's the baby's name, girl, he's——'

Her eyes snapped open in response to Steele's softly-spoken, Southern-accented words. And in the part of a second it took for this to be completed, her expression altered from despair to terror. She squeezed her eyes tightly closed again. Pleaded despairingly:

'No more! Please, I can't! It hurts me so! Please, I beg of you!'

Steele had been standing over her. A man of just a little more than five and a half feet tall with a lean build. More than forty years old and looking every day of his age: this not just because almost all his one-time red hair had greyed. That had happened prematurely. The years and much harsh experience crowded into their passing had burnished and roughened the texture of his features—which right now showed no sign that he could look boyish if he expressed a particular brand of grin. It was a face that had started out with a kind of nondescript handsomeness, and maturity had improved on this. Coal black eyes predominated, and the strength of character they emanated acted to counterbalance the gentleness of the mouthline that might otherwise have given his face a weak cast. He was clean-shaven but wore his sideburns long.

The style of his clothing was that of a dude: albeit one who had fallen on hard times. A grey Stetson with a black, tooled leather band. A cream vest over a white shirt.

9

Blue-black pants that matched the jacket now folded beneath the head of the dying girl. Black riding boots that were spurless and worn under the cuffs of his pants. Around his neck in the manner of a kerchief was a silken scarf and on his hands were black buckskin gloves.

All his clothing was old and stained and some of it was a little threadbare. He carried no discernible weapons. And if the girl sprawled out at his feet could have seen him clearly—and seen, too, the dilapidated hay wagon with its assortment of freight—she would probably have presumed him to be a down-on-his-luck gentleman farmer forced away from his land. Which, Adam Steele reflected fleetingly, was close to the truth.

But he guessed that in her tormented mind she saw him in silhouette against the brightening Californian sky: monstrously tall and featureless, which powered from out of her memory images of what had happened to her before agony and anguish drove her through hysteria into senselessness. And he dropped to his haunches. Waited for her voice to thicken until it was no longer possible for her to force out further entreaties for mercy. Then made the effort to keep his own voice low and gentle in tone when he assured her:

'I'm not one of those who hurt you. I found you just now. Your baby's fine. Just sleeping. Would you like a drink of water?'

She cracked open her eyes tentatively this time: like she was afraid the afternoon light would lance blindingly into them. And if she could not see clearly she would not be able to recognise if he was telling her the truth. She even withdrew a hand from beneath the covering coat and shaded her eyes.

'You're not one of them,' she confirmed to herself. And swallowed hard. 'I don't want nothin' exceptin' for my baby, sir. I have to see my baby?'

Her face augmented the beseeching timbre of her voice,

and only now did Steele realise what a beautiful woman she would have become had she been spared to reach maturity.

'Sure,' he promised, and recapped the canteen. Set it down on the ground and rose to go bring the infant.

She tried to lift and turn her head to watch him, but lacked the strength even for this. Her eyes were drawn to the limits of their sockets, though, so she saw him with the baby at the first opportunity. But when she tried to reach upwards with the hand that had shaded her eyes, her arm fell weakly back to the ground. Tears that had nothing to do with physical pain welled up in her eyes and spilled over the lids: to cut fresh tracks through the dust that adhered to her finely-sculptured cheeks.

Steele lowered himself slowly down onto one knee. Turned and held the tiny child in such a way that the girl was able to see his contentedly sleeping face between the bonnet and the shawl.

A sob shook the girl's punished body and she winced in response to the vicious bolt of pain that was triggered from her horrific wound. Then she found the strength to fist the blurring tears from her eyes so that she could see the infant clearly. Next, incredibly, she was able to show a warm smile of satisfaction that for perhaps five entire seconds conveyed she had peace of mind.

'Babies are the kind of people I don't know too much about, girl,' Steele told her evenly when he saw her brief moments of freedom from despair had come to an end. 'But I reckon this one will be better off left to sleep his fill over on the patch of grass where I found him?'

She swallowed hard, reluctant to agree that the infant should be taken out of her sight. But then she made a barely perceptible affirmative gesture with her head, tried to augment this with words, but found it impossible to voice them. Tears glistened in her eyes again, and squeezed out through the lids even when she had closed them.

Steele returned the baby to the soft ground at the fringe of the stand of pines, already more confident in the way he carried him. But doubt fastened a grip on him when, after he had set the infant on the grass, the tiny face was transformed by a frown and a small cry vented from the pouting mouth. And Steele froze in the act of straightening up, held his breath and willed the dying woman and the horses at the wagon not to make a sound. Then, when the baby was peacefully asleep again, he made a conscious effort to turn and move away with as little noise as possible. Even though he knew he was merely postponing the inevitable.

'Thank you, sir. I am sorry to cause you this trouble.'

She had seemed to be unconscious again, but breathing more regularly, until he lowered himself on to his haunches at her side once more. And she spoke before she opened her eyes—like she felt the need to convince herself of her true feelings before she trusted her eyes to express them.

'It was little enough, girl,' he answered.

'I would like a little of the water you offered, sir.'

He nodded, uncapped the canteen and held it to her mouth so that the water trickled slowly over her lower lip. She swallowed just a minuscule amount before her eyes signalled it was enough.

'My name is Rosebud Petrie, sir. Zachery is my son.'

'Adam Steele, Mrs Petrie. There's not much more I can do to make you comfortable.'

'You've done more than you had to, Mr Steele. And if it matters, I ain't no married lady. It's Miss Petrie.'

Steele took a drink of water himself and closed up the canteen. Said: 'It makes no difference to me, girl.'

'Guess not, Mr Steele. But I know I'm gonna meet my maker pretty soon now. And I wouldn't want to do that knowin' that one of the last things I done on this earth was to deceive a good man that helped me in need.'

She peered intently up at him and if she was feeling any pain now she concealed it perfectly. For all he could read in her handsomely negroid features was a fervid plea for him to believe in her sincerity.

His expression remained impassive when he told her: 'I saw the way you were cut. You've lost more blood than——'

'I know, Mr Steele. If it was just me, maybe I'd be scared to die. I'm only nineteen. Maybe I'd like you to tell me I've got a chance. But . . . oh, dear God in heaven!'

She gaped her mouth wide and vented a muted choking sound. Then her legs jerked up and she wrenched her head to the side on the improvised pillow. And a piercingly shrill scream burst out from deep inside her as she sought relief from a bolt of excruciating agony.

Steele experienced a debilitating sense of impotence in the presence of such a degree of suffering. And the next instant felt relieved when he heard the baby crying. He dropped the canteen he had been holding in both hands and made to rise: sure he was better equipped to calm the infant which had been frightened into waking than to comfort his agonised mother. But, suddenly, he was forced to remain down in the squat. For Rosebud Petrie had thrust forward a hand and fastened a tight fist around his wrist. Continued to scream for a stretched second more. Then by a massive effort of will was able to curtail the sound. Held her breath. As did Steele hold his. And the horses in the wagon traces were equally silent in the wake of their snorts and whinnies while the scream had filled the afternoon.

Only the tiny baby, wailing with uncomprehending fear, disturbed the stillness. Before the pain-wracked young black woman gasped:

'Zachery . . ? Please . . ? Take him . . . In the name of God, I beg you . . .'

13

Then she died.

At one instant her hand gripped his wrist with such force that he felt pain. And on her face was an expression of almost vibrant intensity. While her body was formed into a rigid curve beneath the sheepskin coat. In the next instant the strength was gone from her hand, her body went limp and her face was a grotesque waxen mask: lifeless in the way the dark eyes were glazed and the mouth hung slackly open.

One of the horses scraped at the hard, dust-powdered ground with a forehoof. The other tossed his head up and down. The baby ran out of breath and was blessedly silent for the second or so before he gathered fresh air in his lungs to power a renewed assault on the tragic stillness. Steele gently removed the dead hand from his wrist and lowered it to the ground. Sighed as he straightened up from the corpse and swung away from it to go toward the timber. Glanced skywards and cracked his eyes to a first shaft of sunlight from behind a dark cloud as he growled:

'If you're still listening, how come I always get left holding the baby?' Then he went down on his haunches again, tenderly picked up Zachery Petrie and showed a wan smile when the infant at once stopped crying. Next the tiny face was spread with a smile that put a sparkle in the tearless eyes and showed two miniature teeth in the upper gum. And Steele told him wryly: 'Okay, little man. I reckon I've still got some milk of human kindness in me. But it won't be no use unless your Ma weaned you.'

14

2

At first the Virginian attempted to encourage Zachery back to sleep: by rocking him gently in his arms and then by humming a tuneless lullaby. But the round eyes continued to sparkle as brightly as ever and after a while the near toothless mouth began to issue gurgling sounds that Steele heard as infantile laughter at his efforts.

Several times then he tried to set the baby down on the grass but on each occasion the pleasant gurgling sound was curtailed and Zachery gave vent instead to insistent howls of protest. Eventually, Steele and the team horses became resigned to the ill-tempered noise and while the animals remained patiently docile in the traces, the man began to make preparations to bury Rosebud Petrie. But then as he started to move between the wagon and the timber and the spot where the black woman had breathed her last, he realised the baby could be kept blessedly quiet by something other than holding him. Zachery was apparently fascinated by the mere sight of the Virginian.

Once Steele discovered this, a degree of peace was again brought to the now brightly sunlit afternoon. For by arranging his heavy sheepskin coat against the base of a pine trunk he was able to lodge the baby in a half sitting attitude. And from this position the sparkling eyes in the shiny black face could follow his every move as he dug a shallow grave in the relatively soft ground at the side of the stand of timber.

Then he placed the naked and mutilated body of Rosebud in the hole. Next infilled the displaced dirt on the unshrouded corpse. Finally pushed a fallen tree bough into the newly-dug earth at the head of the grave to serve as a marker.

The baby gurgled a lot during the burial of his mother. And these sounds of glee from an innocent child unaware of what was taking place served to keep Steele from dwelling for more than a few moments at a time on the trouble he was taking on account of a total stranger: and the difficulties beyond mere manual labour that lay ahead of him because of the happy baby who brought a smile to his own lips every now and then.

After he was through with the chore, Steele walked away from the grave without speaking any form of words for the soul of the fine-looking young woman who was buried there. He stowed the shovel back aboard the wagon and then retrieved his jacket-become-a-pillow and put it on before he went to get Zachery Petrie. But pulled up short and frowned.

This was no ordinary passenger that fate had forced upon him. Already Steele had realised there would be a feeding problem in due course. But right now there was another difficulty—a baby of just a few months old could not merely be set down on the wagon seat, nor even be placed carelessly among the freight in the rear of the rig. For his own benefit, Zachery had to be made as comfortable as possible for the rough ride ahead. And if riding in some degree of luxury kept the baby happily quiet, then it would be to the Virginian's advantage, too.

And so the departure of the hay wagon was further delayed, while Steele fashioned a crib directly in the back of the seat. This was comprised of a hope chest with the lid folded completely open, half filled with feed hay on which his sheepskin coat was spread like a mattress. A bed blanket served as a sunshade, two of its corners tied to each end of the seat backrest and the other two similarly fixed to the legs of an upended pine table.

Set down in the crib, Zachery gurgled his approval. And Steel told him in relieved tones:

'It was real lucky I'd started to set up home before the baby came along, little man.'

Then he had to climb down over the high side of the hay wagon and haul himself up on to the seat by way of the spokes of a front wheel. Zachery let out a few howls of malcontent while the Virginian was out of his sight: began to blow bubbles when he could see the man again, albeit partially obscured by the sunshade and the backrest of the seat.

For just a few seconds after he had unwound the reins from around the brake lever, Steele considered steering the two grey geldings into a tight turn to go back the way he had come here. He knew that within two hours of easy travel he would reach a trail. Southward along the trail there was just mile after mile of uninhabited desert. But to the north lay a vast expanse of mountains, their lower slopes cloaked lushly with the timber and brush, wild flowers and grasses that signalled the richness of the soil that was adequately watered. The existence of the trail showed that more than just an occasional traveller had come in off the desert and headed into the verdant high ground. And some would surely have called a halt and put down roots not too far up the trail.

Which notion had caused Adam Steele to turn off the trail and head across a tract of country that was a whole lot less likely to have been settled. But now the circumstances were different. He had been wrong to think there would be no other human presence in this neck of the woods.

And his forfeit for making the mistake was the responsibility for the welfare of an orphan baby.

Well, the hell with changing his plans more than necessary because of his unwanted passenger! He was again briefly the victim of the kind of ill-humour that had brought an occasional scowl to his face while he dug the grave. Then he released the brake and with reins and a soft-spoken command asked the team for an easy walk: straight ahead.

Rosebud Petrie and her tiny son had come from somewhere. So had the three sadists who cut the fatal wound in her. They could have reached here from any point of the compass. Steele knew nothing of this part of California. He could have veered off a trail to nowhere and now be headed toward another that ran through heavily-settled country to link thriving communities. Or what if the nearest isolated farmstead or small town was back on the trail he was driving away from? There was no guarantee Zachery Petrie would be taken in and taken care of. A baby brought in out of nowhere by a passing-through stranger who had buried the infant's young mother somewhere in the wilderness. Worse still, a baby that was black.

Steele, feeling that the scowl was still firmly set on his face, glanced back and had to crane his head to the side to see under the shade blanket and into the hope chest. And for a few moments the scowl became a grin when he saw the baby was more contented than ever. But then it became obvious it was not merely the comfort of the improvised crib and the motion of the rolling wagon that little Zachery was enjoying so much.

'Sonofabitch,' the man rasped at the baby. The baby ceased to blow bubbles and a strained expression showed on his tiny features. Steele said: 'Hey, no offence, little man.' Then sound confirmed what he had already suspected from the smell rising out of the crib. And he halted the rig before returning his only faintly disapproving gaze to Zachery as the infant vented an ill-tempered wail. Told him: 'Sure, sure. I recall what somebody said to me about your kind once. A baby's not much more than a loud noise at one end with no sense of responsibility at the other.'

3

There was one good aspect about cleaning up and changing the tiny baby. It quietened him down again: and he seemed to enjoy more than anything else so far the manner in which he was inexpertly man-handled by the Virginian who scowled his distaste for the chore from start to finish. Steele's humour was not improved by the fact that he had to use pieces of a torn up high quality cotton bedsheet to do the cleaning and replace that item of the baby's clothing he tossed away.

But he was not so repelled by the unsavoriness of the necessary task he failed to notice that Rosebud Petrie had spared no expense in dressing her son. Everything was store-bought not so very long ago, and had cost top dollar. And not only money had been lavished on Zachery. Those articles of clothing which had been worn before had been carefully laundered so they were both spotlessly clean and soft as new.

On the move again, under a now almost cloudless sky, Steele found himself host to a sense of satisfaction at the way he had handled this latest problem posed by his young passenger. And then he felt even easier in his mind after a cautious look beneath the shade blanket showed him that the baby was on the brink of being lulled back to sleep by the smooth progress of the wagon and the muted sounds as hooves thudded and wheels turned on the springy turf of a vast area of grassland. But after indulging himself with such a train of thought for several seconds, he then experienced a stab of irritation at his complacency.

The sun was now closer to the horizon in the west than to the noon-high point of its crawl over the dome of the sky. Probably the baby had not been fed in . . . How long? Steele had found him about two hours ago. It was not possible to estimate how long Zachery had been sleeping there at the fringe of the trees. How long had it taken the men to do what they did to the child's mother?

The frowning Virginian now recalled his sardonic comment that had rhetorically queried whether Zachery Petrie had been weaned or not. For in these new circumstances the answer mattered not at all. If the baby had been raised until now on mother's milk, his supply was curtailed. So what kind of food would be suitable for him . . ?

'The hell with it!' Steele rasped aloud, but his voice was pitched no higher than a rustling whisper. And then he kept the notion that triggered the curse to himself: that the baby would have to take his chances, and that if he was faced for the first time in his life with going hungry then he would quickly learn to eat whatever was available. While if the learning of that lesson meant the man charged with taking care of him had to endure a marathon period of howls and wails, then so be it.

But then, as the Virginian decided that he would solve the potential feeding problem in such a way, he saw something in the far distance that perhaps meant the problem would not be his to solve.

Since swinging around the stand of pines back where he found the mother and baby, Steele had been driving the wagon over a meadow-like expanse of rich grassland that had gradually developed into a broad valley that curved from the west into the north. The ridge of the slope to the right was featured with an extension of the trees beside

21

which Zachery had been made an orphan. While the western side of the valley beyond the grassy bottom land was covered with a forest of mixed timber that spread without a break for as far as the eye could see, the ridge of the slope to the west higher and more distant than that to the east.

At first Steele had considered heading down into the valley and across it when it began the arc northward. For at that point the way west was not so thickly timbered that it looked difficult to traverse. And west had been his elected course until the terrain had briefly enforced a swing to the south. But when he first departed the trail his motive had the logical basis that he wanted to avoid those parts of the country likely to be populated. Now his circumstances were changed. He needed to find people, and he was as likely to do this in the north as the west. And since the going was obstacle-free under the eastern crest of the valley side, he steered this route.

Which took him toward the house.

Afternoon was on the brink of becoming evening when he glimpsed the single-story, stone-built house with windows that glinted in the still-warm rays of the sinking sun, light that had not yet begun to change colour from yellow to red. It was perched on an outcrop of rock that jutted from the ridge, and in back of it was a clearing in the timber that he thought had not been there before somebody decided to site the house in this particular spot.

An idyllic spot, Steele thought: and not without envy. For it commanded a magnificent view across a vast tract of land that was rich in many shades of green—be it grass or trees—which was as yet untouched by the caring hands of a man who could respect such country as he put it to good use. Such a piece of land as he had been looking for ever since . . .

He made the conscious effort to check this line of thought as he drove the wagon close enough to the house to hear a regular thudding sound from the clearing out back of it. This as he saw smoke begin to wisp from the chimney. And was briefly angry at himself on two scores. First that he had been so preoccupied with his charge that he had failed to see at the outset that this valley was perfect for his purpose. Second that to think of it so was a futile exercise anyway: since somebody else had already set down roots here. Then he made another conscious effort: to bar from his mind any inconsequential notions— particularly those that could be termed dreams, wishes or hopes. He had gotten beyond the stage of needing to indulge in wistful musings. The wagon and its freight— Zachery Petrie apart—amounted to material evidence of that.

After the cadence of the thudding had slowed, faltered and then ceased, Steele recognised what the sound had been. The bite of an axe blade into timber. Then, as the axe was swung again, he thought he detected the clean fragrance of fresh-cut wood. This just before the more acrid taint of burning wood became dominant in the evening air: the smoke rising densely from the chimney now.

Because the house was built on the promontory of granite that jutted out from the ridge, there was no access to it from the front. Nor at the south side, where Steele approached: unless by way of a difficult climb through an expanse of thorny brush and nettles that clung to the near-sheer final rise of the valley at this point. So he had to drive the wagon on by the house, passing some sixty feet below its west-facing wall, in which the two windows now reflected a red sun.

Beyond the wedge of grey rock, the grade to the timbered top of the valley side was less steep and the springy turf extended to the fringe of the pines. But the slope was still too much for the laden wagon with just two average size geldings in the traces. On foot it was an easy climb for Steele, even carrying the still-asleep baby in his arms.

At the top he could see the house had not been here very long, and that he had been right in his guess about the clearing behind being man-made. And a man was still working in the final light of the day's end at felling trees to extend the open area that right now was some hundred feet wide and twice that deep. He had taken another rest while Steele was coming up the slope, but now began again to swing a long-handled axe at a gaping wound in the base of a tall pine. The tree was being cut to fall into the clearing, alongside three others that had been trimmed of their branches. A blackened area of dirt showed where the waste of felled trees was burned. Another, much larger area, had been dug over. A short run of fencing had been erected along one side of the clearing, and a large stack of fence poles was ready to be set up in due course. Midway down the clearing on the side where fencing had not yet been commenced there was an outbuilding of new timber freshly treated with creosote.

The aromas of woodsmoke, cut timber and creosote were merged in pleasant combination. And then Steele found himself enjoying the atmosphere even more as he neared the house and the tantalising smell of roasting meat reached out through the open doorway toward him.

This doorway was close to the corner in the north-facing wall of the house which was a dozen feet back from the edge of the outcrop. A three-feet high wall of the same stone used to build the house was in process of being constructed to guard the edge of the sheer drop that started out at the top as a matter of inches, but rapidly increased to dangerous dimensions.

A rutted, wagon-wide track began at the ridge side of the promontory and wound over a meandering course through the timber to the north east of the clearing.

The Virginian assimilated his first impressions of the

24

place in the few moments it took him to cross the smooth rock from the top of the slope to the doorway. And at the same time decided not to call out to the tall, leanly-built man in dark-hued coveralls who was swinging the axe with an action that was smooth but nonetheless suggested the work was wearying him. Zachery Petrie was undisturbed by the regular thud of sharp steel into pine wood, but a raised voice would surely wake him. The woman's voice, though, was muted when she asked:

'Goodness, what do you have there, mister?'

She was not startled. Instead, it was Steele who was surprised by the manner in which she moved silently on to the threshold of the doorway as she put the question.

'Ma'am,' he acknowledged, and held the baby more firmly in the crook of an arm so he could raise a gloved hand to tip his hat. 'Do you know anything about babies?'

'Babies?' Now she was surprised. Kept her feet rooted to where she stood as she leaned forward from the waist. First shot a glance across the clearing to where the man was working. Then tried to take a closer look at the infant in Steele's arms. There was apprehension in her manner, like she was concerned she was doing something wrong. 'I figured that was a baby that you was carryin', mister. From the way you was holdin' the bundle. Ain't nothin' . . . I ain't never had no baby. Had a little baby sister once that I used to take care of every now and again when my Ma was busy.'

She was a full-bodied woman who was just an inch or so shorter than Steele. She was no more than twenty-five years old and she had been brassily beautiful: would be so again when the dark coloration and the swelling had disappeared from beneath her right eye. An older bruise on the left side of her neck would soon have faded completely, but this injury would not have detracted from the round attractiveness of her even-featured face when it had been more prominent. She had dark eyes, full lips and

a pale complexion that was naturally unblemished. Her
hair was long and fine and fell to below her shoulders
in the kind of waves that looked best when it was unruly.
Its colour was too obviously blonde, and so was probably
dyed. She wore a flame-red dress that by its cut and white
trimming looked like a ball gown. Its full skirt was covered
at the front by a floral-patterned apron tied around her
nipped-in waist. The bodice hugged her high, conical breasts
and a row of close-set buttons clearly defined the deep
valley between them.

Steele was briefly disconcerted by running across such
a fine looking young woman dressed in such a manner
in a place like this. And was suddenly aware that several
stretched seconds had elapsed since she had finished
saying her piece in a carelessly uncultured accent.

'You know something about feeding a baby young as
this one, ma'am?' he asked, feeling foolishly tongue-
tied as she gazed at him, her apprehension suddenly
tempered by feminine pride that her appearance had
unsettled him.

'How old's that?'

'Six months, I reckon. No more.'

'Don't you know?' She even smiled now. Just the
merest suggestion of the kind of happiness she could
express in better circumstances. But although her full lips
were parted to display white and even teeth and there was
a slight sparkle in her eyes, nagging worry was obviously
undermining her desire to enjoy the situation.

'He's not mine, ma'am. As you can see.'

'Can't see much of anythin' now it's near dark,' she
countered.

And she made to step out of the doorway. But suddenly
she swayed back and withdrew her foot. And the fraction
of a smile was gone from her bruised face as she vented a
tiny cry of alarm. This as the final thud of axe blade into
wood was followed by the drawn-out wrenching sound

26

of the trunk tearing itself away from its stump. Then the rushing of air through foliage as the impetus of the toppling pine increased. Finally the crash of its entire length as it impacted with the ground.

Then the wails of Zachery, frightened awake, could be heard.

And the woman rasped urgently: 'You have to say you just this moment got here, mister!'

The man was saying something, too. But just the sound of his voice reached incoherently across the length of the clearing until he had hurried closer to the house: moving with the gait of somebody suffering pain. '. . . me, I tell you! Who the hell are you? What d'you want here on our place?'

He had been gesturing with the long-handled axe at the start of his clumsy half-run. But then he needed to use it as a walking cane after he almost pitched to the ground. Belligerence remained firmly fixed on his face, though, as he now hobbled forward.

'——most jealous man in the whole of creation,' the woman was saying, her voice a whisper but its tone insistently earnest. And when Steele spared her a glance he saw the intense expression on her face emphasised the warning she had voiced.

'Answer me, man! This here's private property! You have no right to come here unless invited! Stop that brat from screaming, can't you?'

Steele had begun instinctively to rock the baby as soon as the explosion of sound from the falling tree had brought him noisily awake. He continued with the same easy swinging motion as he glanced back into the doorway, which was abruptly empty. Then looked toward the furious man who had advanced to within a dozen paces. And rasped in a harsh whisper just loud enough to be heard above the now less shrill complaints of Zachery Petrie:

'That's what I'm trying to do, feller. Maybe it would be easier if you were to keep a little quieter and——'

'Nobody tells me what to do on my own place, stranger!' the man cut in as he came to a halt a few feet back from the corner of the house. And breathlessness from anger and exertion acted to mute his voice.

'Just a suggestion,' Steele said, and half turned away from the doorway, to keep the light out of the baby's eyes as a lamp was lit against the dusk.

'What is it you want here?' the woman asked and her tone was close to being merely curious. This as part of a charade that was meant to fool the man into thinking there had been no earlier exchange at the threshold of the house. 'I'm Mrs Murchison and this here is my husband, Clay. We've gotten to be a mite suspicious of strangers, livin' out here like we do. Clay sometimes is——'

'Shut your flappin' mouth, Chrissy!' Murchison snarled. And was able to power the command forcefully after he had sucked in several deep breaths while the woman addressed the Virginian.

She stood just inside the doorway, holding the newly-lit lamp, and on her face was an entreaty that tacitly pleaded with Steele not to antagonise her husband. Steele went along with what she wanted: made the effort to check an urge to anger that the irascible man had triggered in him.

'Came by this orphan earlier today,' he told Murchison in even tones. 'I need some advice on how to take care of him.'

Clay Murchison was twice the age of his wife. He was close to six feet tall and was skinny rather than lean. But there was something about his rangy frame that suggested he had been powerfully built in his younger days. And ruggedly handsome, too: whereas now his leathery textured face was haggard—the blue eyes sunken, the cheeks hollow and the mouth slack. The full head of jet black hair looked strangely out of context—almost like the strength of its

28

growth had sapped the man's energy and caused his wasted, used-up appearance. Bristles grew thickly, too, on his lower face and throat.

He had worked long and hard today and had sweated a great deal; then ingrained the dirt of his chores into his sparse flesh when he wiped away the sticky and salty moisture. But freshly washed up and shaved, and wearing his Sunday best clothing after a good night's sleep, Clay Murchison would still look drained of almost all his stamina—sustaining himself from a rich reserve of will-power not to be beaten.

He suffered physical pain, also: for his angry scowls were often transformed momentarily into grimaces of discomfort even after he halted his hobbling, axe-assisted advance across the clearing.

'We don't know nothin' about no brats here, stranger,' he growled as he ran the back of a hand over his dirty, sweat-beaded brow. 'Me and Chrissy don't have none.'

He seemed to be as relieved as the Virginian that the baby had quietened and now just uttered a series of irregular, irritable cries. For although the glower on his gaunt face conveyed he was still in high anger, he forced himself not to raise his voice.

'Clay, I had to tend to my little sister Jenny when I was——'

'Get back to tendin' to my supper, Chrissy,' her husband commanded with low-toned insistence.

'Milk. We can spare some milk. It's what little babies have.'

Steele looked at Chrissy Murchison and saw the genuine concern and desire to help on her bruised face. Then swung his head to meet the sullen gaze of the man as he allowed sourly:

'So all right. Give the stranger some of our milk. So he and the brat can be on their way. Leave a work-wearied man in peace to eat his supper.'

'I'll get it,' his wife said quickly, drawing the Virginian's attention back to the doorway as she swung out of sight again. And for the first time he took passing notice of that part of the room visible to him beyond the threshold. Saw it was a small parlour, furnished for comfort without luxury. Immaculately clean and with a faint scent of polish discernible against the predominant fragrance of roasting meat that permeated into the room from the kitchen. Just a single odd note was struck by an aspect of the decoration in the comfortable country parlour. This the way in which a lawman's silver star and a matched pair of Remington revolvers were displayed on the white washed wall above the fireplace in which the makings of a fire were laid.

'Be best if you didn't look like that at the way Chrissy moves, stranger,' Murchison advised with low-toned menace.

And it was Steele's turn again to check the impulse to anger when he saw the wasted and wearied man had taken a two-handed grip on the axe: his stance an aggressive extension to his voice and expression.

'She's not there to see, Murchison,' the Virginian muttered as he continued to rock Zachery gently back and forth. 'If I was staring at anything, it was the sheriff's badge and the fancy pistols.'

'None of that is any of your business, stranger.'

'You're right.'

Murchison gave an emphatic nod and carried the axe one-handed down at his side as he hobbled up to the doorway and stepped into the house. Again he was forced to interrupt the scowl with an occasional wince in response to jolts of pain.

'Was shot in the leg one time,' he felt compelled to explain, even though there was no enquiry in the cold gaze Steele directed at him as he assumed the place on the threshold vacated by his wife. 'Bothers me some after a long day workin' the place.'

30

'Man has to take the rough with the smooth,' the Virginian drawled. Talking for the sake of it since it seemed that Zachery Petrie was now less inclined to complain of his hunger when he could hear voices.

'I wouldn't know, stranger. On account of I don't figure I ever had the chance to compare one with the other.' He looked set to elaborate with a tale of woe, but the footfalls of his wife intruded into the train of his embittered thought and he turned toward her to demand: 'Here, give it me. You pour me a big one and then see supper's on the table by the time I've washed up.'

'Clay, I should tell——'

'Do like I *tell* you, woman!' he snarled. And the way he jerked back his free hand and she vented a soft cry it was apparent he had wrenched the milk-filled bottle painfully out of her grasp. It was a bottle that had once contained rye whiskey and from the way he eyed it as he held it out toward the Virginian, there might still have been liquor in it. 'All right, stranger, there it is. You can be on your way now.'

'It oughta be heated,' Chrissy Murchison hurried to explain. 'Not too hot, mind. When you——'

'Shit, the brat's a black one!' her husband roared, able to see the face of the baby for the first time after Steele leaned forward and took the bottle. 'You get that black sonofabitch off my property right now, you sneaky bastard! If I'd known . . .'

The explosive outburst had triggered a fresh onslaught of shrill howls from Zachery Petrie. And Steele experienced a fear of his own: stepped hurriedly back from the doorway as Clay Murchison took a menacing double-handed grip on the axe again. But abruptly the enraged man swung around to fasten his glinting eyed stare on his wife.

'I didn't know, Clay!' she defended, terrified. 'Honest, I never seen . . .'

Her husband flung the axe to the side and its thud of impact was accompanied by the shattering of china. Thus he had both hands free as he whirled away from the threshold: was able to slam the door violently shut with one hand while the other landed a vicious blow across the face of his wife.

Chrissy Murchison screamed her pain.

Clay Murchison bellowed: 'You know my views on the black scum of this earth, you bitch! You know I want for every last one of them to be put down! Yet you give . . .'

Steele had paused for just a moment after the door crashed into the frame and the woman cried out. Then he turned away from the house of violence in such an idyllic setting and was soon out of earshot of the man who ranted his bigotry. For midway down the steep slope toward the wagon, the slab of rock on which the house was built acted to mute the furious voice. And by that time, too, Zachery Petrie had quelled his own fretfulness to a level which allowed the Virginian to compete without shouting as he told the baby ironically:

'My guess is that she'd have taken you in, kid. But there's no mistaking how he feels about you. You've been black bawled.'

4

For a few minutes that seemed like a lot longer, Adam Steele struggled to get Zachery Petrie to take some of the milk that had been so much trouble to obtain. He sat on the grass with his back against a rear wheel of the wagon and attempted to feed the milk, a droplet at a time, into the baby's mouth that was constantly gaped wide to voice his displeasure.

But either the infant did not think too highly of the milk, or he resented the feeding process which sometimes caused him to choke when the bottle tilted too sharply and the milk was poured rather than dripped.

Then, motivated more by fear that he might cause the baby to drown on the milk than by his mounting ill-humour with the constant howls, the Virginian changed his technique. He returned his squealing charge to the hope chest become a crib and climbed up on to the wagon seat, Poured some milk into his tin cup, took off a glove and leaned over the backrest of the seat. Dipped a finger into the cup of milk and then placed his damp finger into the noisy mouth of the orphan.

Zachery Petrie sucked in silence for a moment. Then started a wail of protest when the milk was gone and just a tasteless fingertip was left: was blessedly silent again for another moment or so after the finger had been dipped a second time.

33

Steele grinned in satisfaction at his own inventiveness, and next developed an improvement on the method of feeding. Held the cup close to the baby's head and had three fingers soaking and ready while a fourth was being used to sustain Zachery and keep him quiet. Fleetingly, the Virginian realised he should have washed his hands. Also, he had neglected to take Chrissy Murchison's advice to boil the milk.

'Times are hard all round, little man,' he told the baby. 'But I seem to recall somebody saying once that all kids are bound to take in a peck of dirt before they grow up. Or something like that.'

Zachery began to make happy sounds and to suck less voraciously: content in the knowledge that one milky finger was inevitably replaced by another. And soon the Virginian was so adept at giving the milk to the baby that he did not have to look at what he was doing. Could shift his gaze from beneath the shade blanket and peer up at that section of the corner of the house that was visible from this point below the promontory. As he did so, the moon suddenly appeared from behind a bank of cloud, threequarters full and bright. Its light dimmed into insignificance the faint glow that reached down to the wagon from one of the house windows. It seemed to be as quiet up there now as it was on the wagon, and in the massive silence that reigned over this vast expanse of timber and grass land, he guessed that a voice raised in embittered anger would reach down to him.

He did not spend too much time gazing up at the house on the rock. Just for long enough to try to justify to himself the part he took in causing the trouble that had led to the beautiful young woman getting another lump from her quick-tempered husband.

He had been ignorant of the jealousy and bigotry of Clay Murchison. And even if he had known something of the darker side of the character of the life-soured man, it was still important to get food for the helpless black baby. While as far as the vicious blow Murchison landed on his wife was concerned . . ? She was no stranger to the violence of the man and must have known there was a danger that she would invite such a response when she argued with him.

Or had she truly not seen that the baby was Negro? Could Adam Steele truly exonerate himself? Not feel guilty because he had used Zachery Petrie as an excuse to turn his back on the woman who helped him?

Hell, that was the way it had happened and there could be no going back, he chided himself. There was now no point in reflecting, after the event, that maybe the un-written rule about not interfering in the domestic strife between a man and his wife was a good one.

He shifted his suddenly baleful gaze to survey the moonlit vista of rich countryside that was spread out on all sides of him. But abruptly brought this to an end and gave the happily feeding baby his full attention the moment he felt the first stab of envious resentment that such a fine piece of land should have been settled by a couple like the Murchisons.

Zachery drank something over a half a cup of milk before he let it be known by the forceful pressure of his tongue that he was through. And Steele wasted little time in getting underway after the eventful halt at the house on the rock outcrop. Looked back just once before the curve of the narrowing and shallowing valley took him out of sight of it beyond intervening timber. When he saw that his instinct for being aware of watching eyes was still sharp for, silhouetted against the rectangles of light in a north facing window was the head-to-waist form of Chrissy Murchison.

He drove the wagon for something close to another two miles before he found a good place to pitch a night camp. This was out of the valley which the Murchison house overlooked. At the head of another that meandered in a generally north western direction. It was more thickly covered by timber on both steeper sides that dropped deeper down to where a stream glinted in the moonlight. The water flowed at a gentle rate and the sounds of it running over a rocky bed were muted to a pleasant, soporific level by distance.

The baby seemed to like the far off gurgling sounds as much as Steele, who made the effort to work quietly at the chores of pitching camp in a richly-grassed glade at the top of the long and easy slope that fell away into the deep valley at its eastern end. For as soon as the horses had been taken out of the traces and hobbled and a fire had been laid, Zachery Petrie began to utter tiny noises that imitated those from the slow running stream below. Because of this, the Virginian held off from lighting the fire and eyed the two horses impassively—willing the animals to stand quietly for as long as it took the orphan infant to be lulled to sleep.

And they did. So that when they began to crop on the grass, the tearing sounds of their feeding competed only with the less obtrusive bubbling of slow-moving shallow water. But Steele waited for perhaps a full minute before he moved to where the baby lay in his sheepskin, propped against a wheel of the wagon so he had been able to watch all that was happening. Then, taking pains not to jar the deeply-asleep Zachery, he returned him to the improvised crib. Used a four-times folded blanket to cover him against the chill of the night that was starting to make itself felt. Was thus able to don the coat to keep warm himself until the crackling fire started to give forth some heat.

Twice as he was cooking some bacon and beans he checked to see that his charge had not turned over into an attitude which might smother him within the hope chest. And then he looked at the sleeping infant again before he poured some coffee from the pot into his cup: was able to sit in a comfortable cross-legged attitude and drink with a satisfied mind. For as a baby-minder it seemed he was doing fine.

The first cup of coffee was in his belly and he was about to pour a second when he heard a sharp crack that was not emitted by the fire that had burned low while he ate the meagre meal; and he experienced satisfaction with his present situation alter to concern about the future. And suddenly apprehension became anger and this in turn expanded to fear. Somebody was in the darkly moon-shadowed timber beyond where the horses were hobbled. The pair of geldings had heard the snap of a dry twig under a booted foot—and abruptly ceased to tear at the grass and were standing with heads high and still, ears pricked.

Because he had been so self-satisfied with how he had handled the responsibility of the baby until now, then started to worry about tomorrow, he had failed to remain alert to the possible dangers of the present. Something he was hardly ever guilty of in normal circumstances. But tonight, as he sat between cups of coffee in the light of a diminishing fire and a bright moon, he was all-but helpless while someone watched him from the darkness. For his rifle was far out of reach, up on the wagon beneath the seat. And he was armed only with the silken kerchief which had weighted corners to make it into a weapon of strangulation, and the knife that he carried in a boot sheath strapped to the outside of his right leg.

The horses set back their ears and dipped their heads to begin cropping at the lush grass again. But Steele's sense of being surreptitiously watched remained strong. So he stayed as tense as ever behind an outwardly casual attitude: forcing fear to act as a sharpening effect on his instincts and reflexes as he eased a gloved hand inside the slit in his pants leg to touch the knife.

37

'Mister!' a woman's voice called, soft and fearful. And Steele fisted his hand around the handle of the knife. 'It's me, mister! Chrissy Murchison! If you tell me to leave, then that's what I'll do!' He had started to draw the knife from the sheath while his mind was filled with the near hallucinatory notion that the beautiful young woman with the too-yellow hair was being used by her husband to trick him. 'Honest I will.'

Now he vented a soundless sigh and felt most of the tension drain out of him as he relaxed his grip on the knife handle but did not withdraw his hand. Said: 'Mrs Murchison, come out into the light.'

She did so. Made a great deal of noise: with the strain of breathless breathing and the swishing of the full skirts of the elaborate gown that she still wore beneath a thick coat that she could button only down to the waist. She advanced around the horses which were now indifferent to her presence, and came to a halt some ten feet from the fire before she spoke.

'I'm sorry if I startled you, mister.'

'Don't apologise, ma'am,' Steele told her earnestly as he removed his hand from within the purpose-made slit. 'You just gave me a fresh lesson on a subject I was getting a little stale on. I'm grateful to you.'

His voice sounded slightly strained to his own ears, but he thought this could be a final after-effect of those moments of anger and fear that had created a dream-like quality out of his sense of vulnerability.

'I don't get you, mister. But it don't matter much to me. I'm pretty damn dumb about most things. I guess you bein' grateful to me about somethin' means you don't want me to leave right away?'

Her shoulders were sloped low, her hands were thrust deep into the pockets of the coat and there was a stricken expression on her bruised face that in combination conveyed the degree of dejection that she truly felt. While

38

with her tone of voice she seemed to be trying to pretend she could easily rise above whatever brand of mistreatment she might receive at the hands of this stranger.

'Would you like some coffee, Mrs Murchison?' Steele asked, holding up the cup.

'Thanks, but no thanks.' She took another two paces closer to the fire. Halted and took a hand from a pocket. Raised it to touch the tips of her elegantly long fingers to the new discoloured swelling at the centre of her left cheek. Added: 'One thing, mister.'

'What's that, ma'am?'

'I ain't blamin' you for this. Clay ain't never needed no more excuse than supper bein' late to the table or me sayin' the wrong thing at the wrong time—innocent like—to beat up on me. Especially when he's drunk or work-weary or his aches are painin' him.'

'I'm glad, Mrs Murchison—that you don't attach any blame to me and the baby. Sit down awhile?'

'How is the baby?'

'He's asleep in the wagon.'

She nodded absently, then had difficulty sitting down on the ground in the full-skirted ball gown, but managed it, one hand still in a pocket. On the opposite side of the fire from Steele.

'It's a cold night.'

'He's warm enough to be sleeping easy, Mrs Murchison.'

Her expression had started to soften as she relished the warmth of the fire. Then abruptly she showed a different brand of worry to before as she blurted: 'Goodness, I didn't mean to tick you off nor nothin' like that, mister. I bet you've taken real good care of the little one.'

'The milk helped.'

'Oh yeah, I almost forgot. I was hopin' I'd catch up with you. Here, I got some more for him.' She withdrew her hidden hand from its pocket to bring out another pint liquor bottle filled with milk.

'Grateful,' Steele acknowledged and poured himself the delayed second cup of coffee when she set the bottle down on the grass at her side.

She wriggled in a little closer to the fading heat of the dying fire and extended both her hands to the flickering flames. They were trembling and twice she shuddered. But as Steele sipped the coffee he felt sure it was not the coldness of the night air that made Chrissy Murchison do this. She was afraid.

He allowed her the opportunity to think through her troubles in light of the circumstance that he had not turned her away from his camp. But when this started to take a dangerously long time he set down his cup and rose to his feet. The unhurried move startled her out of her frowning reverie, but she was less tense again after a short gasp, when she saw he went toward the wagon. Then was as distraught as before when she saw him turn away from the rig, the rifle from beneath the seat held down at his side.

'Goodness, what's the matter?' She made the demand in a strangled whisper.

When he was seated on the ground across the fire from her again, the rifle at his side, and had taken another sip of coffee, he answered: 'I owe you, Mrs Murchison. For the help in need. You can tell me what you want in return when you want to. But meantime your husband could show up carrying a grudge and something that has a longer range than a timber felling axe.'

'Goodness!' She snapped her head from side to side, looking back over each shoulder in the direction from which she had approached the camp. Then composed herself before she assured: 'Oh, I don't think there's anythin' to worry about concernin' Clay until mornin', mister. He was passed out drunk and snorin' fit to wake the dead when I left the house. Saw off a bottle and a half without hardly touchin' his supper. I've seen before what that kinda drinkin' without no food in his belly can do to Clay.'

'I reckon you don't plan on being back home before he knows you've left?' Steele questioned.

'Damn right!' she answered with low voiced vehemence. 'Long gone is where I plan on bein' when that sonofa . . . when that brute of a husband wakes up.'

Her dark eyes glittered in what remained of the firelight's glow: challenging the Virginian to take issue with her decision.

'You want to ride with me, Mrs Murchison?' he asked evenly.

She had to take a deep breath before she was able to confirm: 'I know it seems like a whole lot to ask in return for some lousy milk, mister. And if you have to turn me down, I won't think so bad of you. Trouble between married folks didn't oughta drag in outsiders. And anyways, Providence ain't so far for a girl to walk to. Just five miles from the house and I already covered best part of half that distance, I guess.'

'Providence is a town?'

She nodded. 'Not much of one.'

'You have friends there?'

She vigorously shook her head and spread a grimace across her bruised face. 'I don't have friends anywhere anymore, mister. Not since I got hitched to Clay Murchison.'

'You already said that's none of my concern, ma'am.'

'Right. Right. No, mister—hey, can I call you somethin' else except for just mister all the time?'

'Name's Adam Steele.'

'Adam all right? And if you wanna call me Chrissy, it's fine with me. Christine is the whole thing, but that kinda sounds almost as formal and unfriendly as ma'am.'

'Whatever you say, Chrissy,' Steele said and finished his coffee. Took the pot off the warm grey embers and asked: 'You sure you don't want what's left?'

'Thanks, but no thanks,' she said again, her composure increasing by the moment. 'I really don't want any. And I really don't wanna take advantage of your good kindness to me overmuch, Adam.'

He shrugged and upended the coffee pot so that its contents hissed and steamed in the almost-out fire.

The woman hurried on: 'Just your say-so to stay here with you until mornin' is all I want. First light is all. Then, if you don't wanna give me a ride the rest of the way into Providence, I'll make my own way there on foot. See, I know it sounds crazy for a full-grown adult like me, but I'm real scared of the dark, Adam. It especially scares me way out here in the country.'

'I'll be moving on soon after sun-up,' he told her as he rose to his feet. 'Room on the wagon for another passenger. And if Providence is any kind of town, I reckon that's where I'll be heading. Maybe find somebody to take in the baby.'

She nodded eagerly. 'Maybe you'll be able to do that, Adam. What I want in town is the stage depot. Figure to take a ride back to San Francisco.'

'That's quite a ride,' he said as he returned the pot and cup to the wagon. And took the opportunity to check that Zachery Petrie was still safely asleep.

'Almost three hundred miles,' she agreed as she came up beside him. 'But Clay has plenty of money in the Providence Bank. And I'll be able to take out enough to buy the ticket. No more than that and a little to take care of eatin' on the way. Once I get to Frisco . . .' She shrugged, then seemed to become aware of the kind of freight the hay wagon carried. And asked suddenly: 'You in the house movin' business, Adam?'

'No, it's all my own stuff,' he told her curtly.

'Goodness, I'm sorry, I didn't mean to poke my nose in where——'

'Forget it,' he cut in, and climbed carefully up into the

42

rear of the wagon, moving cautiously to avoid undue noise. And he kept his voice low as he enlarged on the terse response while he re-arranged the freight to clear a space. 'Until a couple of weeks ago it all belonged to a pair of homesteaders who picked a bad place to settle. They were pulling out to go back east when I happened by. Traded the best riding horse I ever owned and added a fair price in money for the wagon and team and some of their household items. Just a bed to sleep in, a chest to keep mice away from the clothes I'm not wearing, a table and two chairs, some books I'll maybe read, two oil paintings I like and a whole mess of bits and pieces including tools for breaking down the soil and tending crops.'

He came down off the wagon, still moving with care, toting a bedroll.

'You don't look the type of man to set up home?' she said, genuinely puzzled. And was quick to add: 'If you don't mind me sayin' so?'

There was a certain weariness in his voice and expression when he explained: 'Reckon to start up a horse ranch, Chrissy. It's what I've been planning to do for a long time. But it was never much more than an idea. You're right. It has been a lot of years since I had roots. With no more than an idea of putting them down again, it was easy to get side-tracked.' He jerked a hooked thumb at the wagon. 'All that makes me feel that I'm committed to getting started with a ranch just as soon as I find a piece of country that's even halfway right.'

'I'm to sleep in the wagon, Adam?'

'Right. I've cleared a space. Some bedding came with the bed. Pillows and sheets and stuff. In a crate under the bed.'

'I really appreciate you doin' this for me, Adam,' she said. And eyed the high-sided wagon with trepidation.

'Here,' he offered, and abandoned the bedroll so that

he could interlock his gloved hands and place them in a position where she could use them as a step. Then, when she was safely aboard, he told her with a quiet smile: 'If Zachery wakes up in the night you'll be closest.'

'It's a deal.'

Then each of them was content to let the talk be interrupted while they prepared their own beds, Chrissy Murchison in the wagon and Steele underneath it. The Virginian was first to be bedded down, having removed just the sheepskin coat to serve as another blanket. His Stetson he rested over his face to keep stray shafts of moonlight out of his eyes. The Colt Hartford revolving rifle shared his bed-roll—lay at his right side so that the frame was under his loosely-draped hand.

The woman took so long to settle for the night that he suspected she was not merely being over conscientious with the bed-making chore: rather, he thought, she was reluctant to end it. And then, when she was finally through and the lengthy series of small movements and accompanying soft sounds had finished, he could sense the state of tension that gripped her.

'Adam?' she asked tentatively after perhaps a full minute in which just the breathing of a man, a woman, a baby and two horses, and the distant sounds of the stream had kept the silence from being absolute.

'Something wrong?' Like her, he did not need to speak above a whisper since there was just the bed of the wagon and a couple of feet of still night air between them.

'Not as far as I'm concerned. But if you figure there is . . . I mean, if you figure what you're doin' for me is worth a whole lot more than a lousy couple of bottles of milk . . . Well, I wouldn't blame you none. And I want you to know I ain't no strait-laced kinda woman. I wasn't no one-man woman before I got hitched to Clay Murchison. And now I'm runnin' out on that sonofabitch, I sure don't have to keep myself just for him no more. Is that right or ain't it?'

Although she kept her voice down, she sounded more fervently enthusiastic about her subject with each word she spoke. And in the pause he sensed her eagerness to have him agree with her conclusion.

'Right, Chrissy,' he told her, and was disconcerted to discover he had to fake a wearied tone.

'But for you I ain't right?' she countered, abruptly dejected.

'It's the time that's not right,' he told her while a physical response only he knew of proved him a liar. 'And the place maybe.'

'So close to home, uh?' she answered, morosely pensive. 'And so soon after me runnin' out on that sonofabitch of a husband of mine?'

'I reckon.'

'And I reckon I respect you for thinkin' that way, Adam,' she said resolutely. 'But I want you to know somethin'. I want you to know . . . If you get the kinda itch that's so bad it just plain has to be taken care of . . . Well, I won't take it amiss if you just have to wake me to——'

'Got you, Chrissy,' Steele interrupted the eager-to-please woman.

'If you figure I come up to scratch, that is?'

'You're the finest-looking young woman I've met up with in a long time,' he assured her.

'I ain't never been one to take without bein' willin' to give in return. And if a person has got what can be given free, it don't cost nothin' to be generous. Seems to me.'

'Chrissy?' the Virginian said, and knew his voice sounded strained.

'Yes, Adam?' she answered. And from the trepidation in her tone, it was apparent she had misunderstood the cause of his tension.

'Could be your generosity is exceeded only by your beauty,' he told her, making an effort to sound light-hearted. 'But for tonight, sleep tight.'

45

5

Adam Steele seldom had any trouble sleeping. For he attempted to sleep only when he was physically tired. Sometimes, for no good reason he was able to define, his sleep was disturbed by troubled dreams. But this did not happen often, since the passing of many years had acted to blunt even his sub-conscious memories of those transgressions that once had weighed heavily on his conscience. Most nights he simply bedded down, drifted into a shallow but restful sleep and awoke when his body and mind were fully refreshed and prepared for the start of a new day.

Unless he was feverishly sick.

Or his instinct for lurking danger warned him to awaken prematurely to face the threat.

The Virginian could not recall the last occasion he had not been able to sleep easy because of his need for a woman.

A woman he knew. His own woman. A woman he knew he could make his own. A woman who was a once-glimpsed stranger to him. A woman conjured up out of an imagination made fertile by desire. Any damn woman!

He felt his features form into a scowl of self-anger as he acknowledged that this was a stupid line of thought to encourage. A man who was hungry would not find his hunger diminished by vivid memories of past meals or reveries of mouth-watering displays of food in store windows or, even more unobtainable, on other men's tables.

Surely it had to be better for a man with a wearied body and an over-active mind to steer his thoughts far away from anything faintly related to the cause of his restlessness?

Recollections of the great Steele Plantation in Virginia. Of riding as a cavalry lieutenant for the Confederacy. Of his father. Of killing for revenge. Of killing men to keep from being killed himself. Of waking up after weeks of being drunk in a Mexican village called Nuevo Rio. Of . . .

It was no use!

The major areas of his mind became as weary as the larger part of his physical being. But whenever he felt a compelling urge to close his leaden eyelids there was a sudden more powerful counter-force to snap them open again. And he would peer up at the underside of the wagon. While his body stirred and hardened and throbbed at an almost painful intensity for as long as his racing mind was free to be filled with vivid images of Chrissy Murchison. Scenes from memory of how she had been at the house on the promontory of rock and then at his night camp. Next a series of obscene fantasies of how she could be if . . .

He squeezed his eyes tightly closed and willed himself to contemplate a future a long way from here. Of a small house and some corrals and meadows. Of bloodstock horses. Gleaming window panes and white painted woodwork. Good smells coming out of a kitchen. Brood mares with strong foals sired by fine stallions. A shadowy figure in the background who would . . .

'Goddamnit to hell!' Steele rasped as his mind dictated he should link the breeding of horses to yet another erotic image of a woman. Never before had he given more than a passing notion to a woman being a part of his planned stud ranch. Yet here and now he saw one. In a shadowed room. Faceless in the gloom, but naked he knew. Beckoning for him to come to her. Not in a wanton manner.

'Adam, what's the matter?' Chrissy Murchison asked, her voice rasping with fear.

'Nothing,' he replied tautly. And felt a deep gratitude toward her: aware that the sound of her voice had thrust him back to reality just an instant before his need for release would have found involuntary outlet into an illusion. 'If your offer's still open?'

'You mean . . ?' she started to say quickly, her excitement expanded by relief that there was no danger.

Steele suddenly realised just how deeply he had been plunged into the disconcerting turmoil of an imagination that ran riot. His hat still covered his face—so he never had been able to peer up with lusting eyes at the underside of the wagon bed.

Next, as he threw aside his coat and blankets and rolled out from beneath the rig, he knew he had slept. Fitfully, perhaps, but in total for a couple of hours or more. He gauged this from the new position of the glittering moon.

But then how much time had elapsed since he rejected the woman, and whether it had been filled with erotic dreams or the obscene workings of a wide-awake imagination mattered not at all. For as he came upright and looked over the side of the wagon, Chrissy Murchison revealed that the fantasy was just moments away from coming true.

For a second, or perhaps two. No more. And even so, she shuddered beneath the covers after she had pulled them down over her again. But this had been sufficient for Steele to see in the brightness of the moonlight that the woman was naked. Above the waist, at least. Her skin cream coloured: and firmly smooth, he was sure. There were no bruises on the flesh of her torso like those on her face. Unless they were hidden in the moon shadow that her full breasts cast.

When she had covered herself after making the eloquently tacit invitation, her exposed teeth seemed to be clenched against the threat of chattering from the cold. But the bright glint in her dark eyes conveyed they were also supposed to be contributing to her smile of happiness right now and excited anticipation of what was to come.

'Real brazen, ain't I, Adam?' she forced out through her teeth. 'But it's the way I am. I ain't never worn nothin' in bed since I was old enough to argue with my folks. Summer nor winter.'

'Whatever makes you comfortable, Chrissy,' Steele told her as he started to climb up on to the wagon. 'I'm easy.'

'I'm not, Adam. I want you to know that. I got good reason for this and I sure wouldn't be ready and willin' to go with just anybody for the reason that I felt the need to——'

In clearing the space for Chrissy Murchison to bed down Steele had needed to rearrange the way some of the wagon's freight was stacked: taking care as he did this not to disturb the sleeping Zachery Petrie. In other circumstances—even in the middle of a deeply moon-shadowed night—he would certainly have spared a thought for the baby and remembered that certain items of household effects had been moved from one part of the wagon to another. But with his mind and body in the grip of lust, and a nakedly willing beautiful young woman only a few feet away from him, the Virginian was concerned with nothing beyond this near perfect circumstance. Until his foot kicked against a china ewer that toppled over and hit a pile of three copper pans that were bounced off the side of the hope chest before being skittered among the legs of two chairs.

Had it been broad daylight the series of sounds that caused the woman to abruptly curtail what she was saying would probably not have seemed unduly obtrusive. Maybe a baby would have slept on through it, even. But in the

49

dead of night the crash and clatter seemed to be amplified out of all proportion. In the same way as the moments of silence aboard the wagon while both Steele and the woman held their breath in the immediate wake of the noise seemed painfully solid as it beat against their straining eardrums.

Then Zachery shattered the unreal peace with a short, plaintive cry. Which a part of a second later developed into a full-throated bellow of bad temper.

Steele and the woman locked gazes, and as he felt his expression of eager anticipation change by quick stages to an irritable frown, he saw her provocative smile become a forlorn look of sympathy.

'What a shit,' she murmured, and just for an instant there was a malevolent glint in her eyes as she craned her head around on the pillow to peer toward the chest from which the howls were emanating.

'We aren't supposed to talk that way in front of an impressionable child,' Steele countered absently, turned toward the chest and stooped to reach in under the shade blanket so he could bring out the baby.

'And folks in the kinda mood we were just then ain't supposed to have the rug pulled out from under them by a bawlin' baby, Adam,' she answered without rancour. Added with a wan grin as she began to rise from the bedding: 'Unless they're married. To each other. Here, let me have him.'

The coat, along with the rest of her discarded clothing had served as an additional cover while she slept. Now she used it to shield her nakedness as she came upright, then put it on. Since she was not wearing the full skirted ball gown it cloaked her adequately from throat to mid-ankle.

Perhaps because of the dark, or the cold, or the manner of his sudden awakening Zachery Petrie had continued to cry without interruption even after Steele had picked him up from out of the chest. And the Virginian felt a sense of relief when he had passed the baby into the outstretched arms of Chrissy Murchison. Even though there was no lessening of the shrill, inarticulate protests.

'Hungry again, maybe?' he suggested without conviction.

'Could be just plain scared,' the woman countered without looking up from the baby as she rocked him in one arm and touched his screwed up face with the fingertips of her free hand. 'Or sick. Or in need of a change. We'll try that first. But you can be gettin' a feed ready in case he's hungry.'

She went down on to her knees and laid the protesting baby on the rumpled bedding. Began to unwrap the shawl from around him as she hummed softly: the lullaby just audible above the cries that were starting to sound breathless.

'I'll get right to it,' the Virginian acknowledged. And turned away from the kneeling woman and the baby who had reduced his complaints to a whimpering sound. Steele's mind was still in a turmoil of frustration and anger and shame and resentment: so it was not readily amenable to recalling where either the part-used or still full bottles of milk had been stowed. But then his irritation with the memory lapse abruptly ended. And he had time to rasp: 'Chrissy!'

Just before a smiling man flanked by two who were scowling announced cheerfully: 'Well, well, well. Certainly does make a guy feel old. The way he keeps comin' upon itsy-bitsy babies in this neck of the woods. Is that so?'

'What I'd like to feel is that there woman that's foolin' with the brat, Denny,' the man to the right of centre growled, his sullen expression unchanged as he continued to gaze fixedly at Chrissy Murchison.

'And what I'd like is some peace and quiet, Stan,' the man at the other end of the line of three muttered sourly.

51

'First a feel of her. Then a piece, Lonnie,' Stan answered. And vented a sound like a laugh while the scowl remained as firm set as ever. 'Noisy or quiet, it won't friggin' bother me.'

They were all about thirty. The man at the centre, named Denny, was something over six feet tall, which made him a head taller than the lusting Stan. The ill-humoured Lonnie was a little under six feet in height. All three wore battered hats with wide brims that shadowed their faces, and each had on an ankle-length coat with the gunbelt slung around the outside. Stan had drawn his revolver and was pointing it negligently in the direction of the wagon. The other two draped their right hands loosely over the butts of their holstered guns.

After he had gained this first impression of the trio of intruders on the night camp, Steele scanned the area in back of them and to the sides. For as far as he was able to see without losing the men from his sight. And while he did this his mind was stripped of all superfluous emotions: except for the inevitable fear of the kind he could use to hone whatever reactions he would be called upon to make.

'There's just the three of us, dude,' Denny explained and Steele felt drawn to gaze at the men to the exclusion of all else again. Peering down at them from his elevated position on the back of the wagon, over a distance of some fifteen feet to where they were aligned at the side of the long-dead fire. 'Me, I'm Denny Parker. This here is Lonnie Ashton. And this is Stan Tait. We've been headin' for here ever since we saw your fire smoke. Maybe three hours ago, I figure.'

Zachery Petrie seemed to be all cried out. Or perhaps it was just that he enjoyed being rocked by the now tensely silent woman while words were traded among the men.

'What the frig is all that to this guy and his missus, Denny?' Ashton asked irritably.

'Shut your mouth, Lonnie,' Parker ordered in the same even tone he had used since he first spoke. And without shifting his attention away from the Virginian. 'I'd say you figure you're nobody's fool, dude. You got that stamp on you. Me and them . . .' he rocked his head from side to side, '. . . we get mistook for suckers most of the time. But you're the one got suckered tonight, uh? Even after the fire smoke was gone, I still knew where you were camped. Had a line on you because of that high point of rock across on the west side of the valley there.' He made another slight gesture with his head to indicate a distant outcrop at the top of the steep slope above the valley with the stream flowing quietly along its bottom land. 'Knew when we got close. So we had to dismount and move in real quiet. Then had some luck, I got to admit. The way you made the ruckus with the pots and pans and that woke the baby. Give us the cover to get to here. Close enough to blast you into hell with our pistols if you give us any trouble.'

'Frig that, Denny!' Tait snarled. 'Blast him now and he sure won't give us no trouble.'

'And you shut your mouth as well, Stan,' Parker demanded of the man who had hardly for a moment shifted his gaze away from Chrissy Murchison.

Only now did Steele realise the men on the ground could see no more than the woman's head and shoulders, for from their angle of vision the rest of her would be concealed by the high side of the hay wagon. But even with such a restricted view, they were able to see she was a young, blonde-haired beauty.

At the same time as he became aware of this less than imperative factor concerning the trio's viewpoint of the woman, he was also host to inconsequential stray images of the men's faces. Features he had glimpsed from time to time as heads were moved so that hat brims for a moment or so failed to drop moon shadows. All of the faces lean and angular, in keeping with the coat-draped frames of the men. Parker had a large, slightly crooked nose and heavily crinkled bags under his eyes. Ashton's left cheek was marked by the livid scar tissue of an old cut that inscribed a perfect curve from the corner of his eye to the side of his mouth. Tait had large teeth that were discoloured and protruded at the top. All the men had not shaved in several days.

'Like I said, had some luck,' Parker went on. 'But don't they say that luck goes with the winners?'

'Hell, Denny, it's a surprise you ever stop yakkin' for long enough to hear what anyone else has to say,' Lonnie Ashton growled.

'You know what I think?' Stan Tait snarled.

'Sure know where you think,' Parker answered and seemed suddenly weary of the situation.

'Right,' Ashton said. 'Everyone knows you're scared to cross your legs, Stan. For fear you could get brain damaged.'

'Screw you, Lonnie,' Tait countered in the same only slightly rancorous tone the other man had used.

'What'd I tell you?' Ashton said.

'I'm grateful for the explanation, feller,' Steele drawled, angry with himself behind the impassive mask of his face that was unshadowed by a hat brim. 'Eases my mind a little.'

His Stetson was still beneath the wagon. Close to the blankets and sheepskin coat that concealed the Colt Hartford. But it was not the fact in isolation of being out of reach of the rifle that stirred his burning anger. Instead, that he had allowed himself to become a victim of these men who could, as one of them had claimed, blast him into hell on the merest whim. They were that close and he was that defenceless. All because of an orphan baby and another man's wife. No! Not even Zachery Petrie and Chrissy Murchison were to blame for putting him into this

54

bind. Circumstances had brought him across their paths and he had elected to accept the options that had led to all three of them being aboard the wagon here and now. He alone was at fault . . . and not for any acts of charity in taking care of a helpless black baby and agreeing to help a woman running away from a brutal husband.

Lust had caused him to drop his guard. Desire for the body of another man's wife. Even after he had rejected her overtures—on the grounds that Chrissy was the wife of Clay Murchison. But not a thought of the life-embittered man passed out drunk in the house on the promontory had even crossed his mind after he surrendered to the compulsion to take the willing woman. Not a thought about any damn thing except the possession of Chrissy Murchison's available, freely-offered young body.

'Why the frig should any of us care about easin' the dude's mind, Denny?' Ashton growled.

'Especially when we could be easin' some other parts of ourselves with that fine-lookin' wife of his,' Tait added. Gave a second terse, harsh laugh.

Zachery was making gurgling sounds of contentment now, while the woman continued to rock him and caress his face. Doing this automatically while she was emotionally detached from the baby as she struggled to contain her terror of the imminent future.

'You're a stupid fool, Stan,' Parker said, in an even tone that extracted spite from the insult. 'The dude ain't. Like I say, I seen the stamp of him. The way he ain't been thrown into no panic by how we crept up on him. How he took the time to check out the rest of what's around here soon as he seen us. He's some smart guy and I like to talk with people who ain't stupid. You guys know that.'

'The reason he don't say so much to you, Stan,' Ashton said, and guffawed.

Tait ignored this to ask with scant interest: 'What makes me a stupid fool this time, Denny?'

'Not knowin' the dude and the blonde with the lumps ain't married.'

'Uh?'

'You can see he was sleepin' under the wagon, Stan. Heap of a bedroll under there, looks like.'

'So they ain't married?' Ashton growled, suddenly more impatient than Tait. 'What the hell difference does it make?'

'Makes the dude a bigger stupid fool than you make me out to be, seems to me,' Tait argued. 'Man that's ridin' with a woman like that who don't make use of her to warm his bed on a night cold as this.'

'My opinion is,' Parker answered thoughtfully, 'he figured that out for himself. And was plannin' on havin' a hot time on a cold night when he tripped over them pots and pans and woke up the kid. Right, dude?'

He was pleased with having worked out what had happened on the wagon before he was close enough to see it: certain he had read it right, but anxious to have it confirmed. He even tightened his grip on the revolver butt as he aimed it at Steele to tacitly demand a response.

'You've got it, feller,' the Virginian supplied, his frustration with the helplessness of his position increasing behind the coolly impassive veneer. The way in which Denny Parker was wasting time with vacuous boasts allowed the Virginian opportunity to consider an escape from this menacing situation. And maybe there was an outside chance for him to get the better of the three men: by going down for the knife, spinning it toward Parker and hurling himself off the far side of the wagon. Then, if Parker's reaction shot missed him, he might be able to drag the Colt Hartford from out of his bedding and start firing before . . .

It was the only plan that entered his racing mind which

56

did not call for some brand of superhuman power: and even it had only the slimmest chance of success. But what if his own luck held, but that of Chrissy and Zachery did not? What if self-survival was at the expense of the lives of an innocent woman and a defenceless baby?

'And you're gonna get it, that's for sure!' Tait snarled. Vented another of his harsh laughs before he added: 'What are you waitin' for now, Denny. The guy's told us all what a smart-ass you are. So now you can blast him and we can——'

'No!' Chrissy blurted, a catch in her voice. Then noisily cleared her throat and got greater force into her tone as she repeated: 'No!'

'No woman tells me no, bitch!' Tait snarled, and made to draw his revolver.

Steele tensed himself to power down into a crouch: to draw the knife from the boot sheath as a first move of a counter-attack that was certain to fail. But if that was the way it had to be, then the risk was worth taking. He was not about to simply stand there and be shot down, irrespective of the danger to the woman and baby. The woman who now rose to her feet, leaving the baby down on the rumpled bedding. This as the enraged Tait snapped his head around to glower at Parker who had thrust out his free hand to grip the wrist of Tait's gun hand.

'Now who's makin' all the noise and ain't listenin' to what other folks are sayin' to him, Stan?'

'I want to make you an offer,' Chrissy said tautly, and momentarily met Steele's quizzical gaze with a look of intense pleading in her eyes.

Ashton started: 'You ain't in no position to——'

'Listen, Lonnie,' Parker advised. And for the first time there was a note of authority in his voice: this emphasising the always obvious fact that he was the top man of the trio. And he felt confident enough of the strength of his command to drop his hand away from Tait's wrist. Then he waved his own revolver in a gesture that invited the woman to end the silence kept from being complete by the far-off trickling of water and the nearby gurgling of Zachery Petrie.

Steele returned his watchful gaze to the men on the ground as the woman beside him on the wagon said:

'Kill Adam Steele and you'll have a hellcat to rape. If that's the way you like to have a woman, I ain't got much else to offer you. Leave him be—and the baby, too—and I'll do anythin' you want. Without no fuss.'

'Sonofabitch,' Lonnie Ashton rasped, a little breathlessly.

Denny Parker licked his lips and when he was done he drew them back to display a wide grin.

Stan Tait vented the shortest of ugly laughs, before he demanded: 'Get on down here and show us what you mean, girl!'

'I ain't that stupid!' Chrissy Murchison snapped, her confidence increasing by the moment. 'Steele and little Zachery stay right here. I go with you. And I'll say when we call a halt and you can have your fun. You ain't gonna have me that way and then be able to kill all of us just——'

'Shit, Denny, this bitch sounds like she's givin' us orders!' Tait snarled, and the spark of enthusiastic interest triggered by the woman's offer was abruptly extinguished by ill-humour.

Parker made a negative gesture with his free hand that drove Tait back into irritable silence and acted to make Ashton bite back on what he intended to say. Then the top man asked of Chrissy: 'What else, little lady? Say we do like you want, and then you do like we want without no fightin' us. We ain't lookin' for no long-lastin'——'

'Money,' she cut in on him. 'In the bank at Providence. Better than two and a half thousand bucks. Account of Clay Murchison. I'm his wife and I can take the money outta the bank with no questions asked.'

'Sonofabitch,' Ashton muttered.

'I ain't never took no money outta a bank unless I was bustin' it out!' Tait growled, suddenly excited by something other than lust.

Parker's voice was as cold as the night air when he instructed: 'I want the both of you down off that wagon. You first . . . Steele, that right?'

'You got it,' the Virginian confirmed as he started to climb out of the rear of the wagon, his throat dry and his muscles aching from the tension that had taken a much firmer grip on his mind and body since Chrissy Murchison had started to propose the deal. Now, as he put his back to the men, he was able to peer up at the woman for more than a fleeting moment. But it was just for a part of a second that she allowed her gaze to meet his. When he saw the depthless extent of her terror that rose close to the surface of her mask of cold composure. Which acted to sharpen his own sense of abject helplessness—and laced it with shame that he could do nothing else but play along with the deal she offered the men.

For now, anyway. Until he could get a hand to the rifle. And at least on the ground he would be closer to it than up on the wagon.

'See, I ain't bothered who I'm with so long as I'm leavin' my husband far——' Chrissy started.

Zachery began to bellow a complaint as the woman made to come down from the wagon and moved out of his line of sight.

'Hey, that sounds just like the black brat we——'

'My guess is it's the same one,' Parker cut in tensely on Tait.

And the knife of anguish was suddenly turned viciously within Adam Steele. Right at the outset of this sinister intrusion on the night camp, Parker had implied that he and the other two men were the sadists who killed Rosebud Petrie. But events of the past were of no consequence to

59

the here and now of imminent new death. Or were they? Men capable of making a woman suffer in the way the pretty black Rosebud Petrie had done . . . Could they be trusted to be bought off by a promise of easy sex and easy money?

Then it no longer mattered: in terms of what Adam Steele could or could not do to save Chrissy Murchison, Zachery Petrie and himself from whatever evil was to be hatched in the minds of these men. For Parker had moved up close behind him as he climbed down from the wagon. Silently until he spoke to Tait. When his voice revealed he was just a few feet away from the Virginian. And Steele was too preoccupied with futile concerns for what had been and what might be: so that he was not even able to think about countering the attack before the barrel of Parker's revolver crashed into the side of his head. Hit him forcefully above his right ear and sent him toppling to the left, air and a groan rushing out of his grimacing mouth. Agony was a searing white heat flaring inside his skull. Then every bone in his frame felt like it shattered as he impacted with the ground. Notions about being even closer to his rifle now came and went from his pain-punished mind. Mixed in with anger at the man who had hit him. Rage at his own incompetence. Shame, too. Pity for the woman. And for the baby.

All this in the dark of a night with no moon. Filled with a rushing sound, seemingly of racing white water, that rose to a deafening volume. Then gradually began to subside. After what seemed to be several long minutes. But it could only have been seconds, he realised, when he cracked open his eyes to capture a blurred visual impression of the scene as his hearing regained crystal clarity.

The distant stream flowing gently in the same unhurried manner as before. Close by the intermittent howls of the displeased Zachery Petrie. Closer still, his own laboured breathing.

Then voices, indistinct at first. Before he heard Lonnie Ashton growl:

'Hard headed sonofabitch, ain't he?'

Then Chrissy Murchison asked anxiously: 'What's he gonna do to him? I told you I'd only——'

Denny Parker cut in, even-toned: 'Stan ain't never been known to kick a man unless he's down.'

Steele knew he had twisted as he fell after taking the stunning blow to his head: lay on his right side. Through the translucence of pain and tears and the lashes of eyes that were barely open he saw four pairs of feet.

The bare ones of the woman who was down from the wagon.

Parker not far from her.

Ashton was still over beside the fire.

Tait was advancing on Steele.

'Please, I beg of you!' Chrissy pleaded.

The degree of Steele's helplessness had swollen many-fold. To the point where he was unable to move a muscle nor utter a sound. And suddenly the horror of surviving totally paralysed was greater than the fear of being kicked to death. He remembered how close he was to the Colt Hartford beneath the wagon. But this realisation served only to sharpen his anguish.

'Hush your mouth, little lady,' Stan Tait rasped as he halted in front of the Virginian and drew back his right foot. 'It seems to me it's this guy that oughta be doin' the beggin'. On account of him being so down . . .' The booted foot swung forward as he completed: 'And out.'

The toe of the boot struck Steele on the jaw. With enough vicious power to wrench his head over with such force that it jerked his body with it. So the Virginian was spreadeagled on his back as he plunged into unconsciousness. Where again time had no meaning in terms of the length of a second, a minute and an hour in the real world.

For it seemed within his disorientated mind that no more than a part of a second had elapsed before he responded to Tait's comment. Murmured huskily:

'If I was a quieter pan handler, I wouldn't be in this mess now.'

6

A man without a trace of compassion in his monotone voice asked: 'What's that you say?'

Steele opened his eyes and snapped them closed immediately. There was a brightly glowing light out there beyond the darkness inside the confines of his skull. And in that brief moment when he looked at it, the intensity of the glow triggered a violent bolt of pain. This pain started out as a tightening and easing grip by invisible fingers on a wad of sensitive tissue inside his head high on the right. After awhile, during the regular intervals of less acute pain while the torturing grip was relaxed, he became aware of a steady burning sensation that was spread across his face from the point of his chin to his temples.

And in his confused brain he abruptly linked burning with fire—this less demanding degree of hurt with the glow of bright light seen when he opened his eyes. Something close to panic took a firm hold on him and every pain was suddenly diminished. Not panic, though: for it was a rational decision to seek escape from death by fire, and only by calm self-control was he able to ignore the pain.

Clay Murchison asked of him: 'You want a cup of coffee, stranger? I ain't brought nothin' stronger with me for this trip.'

There was a fire. But just a small one, built on the ashes

of that which Steele had lit last night. The husband on who Chrissy Murchison was running out sat on a pine chair beside the fire. A tin cup in one hand while the other was lightly curled around the frame of a Winchester rifle that rested across his thighs. The muzzle was pointed in the general direction of the Virginian, but without menace.

'You understand what I'm sayin' to you?' Murchison asked, his tone still devoid of emotion. 'Or did they beat the senses outta you?'

Steele tried to respond, but this seemed impossible. His throat felt like it was filled with sand. But then he was able to gulp clear a passage so he could force out: 'Give me a minute?'

The man with the rangy build and a haggard face who was closer to sixty than fifty at first acknowledged the request with a nod. Then, as he emptied the dregs from the cup and leaned forward to refill it with coffee from the pot, he said: 'They've gone long enough now so that a minute won't make much difference.'

The Virginian did not need to delve into the memory recesses of his aching brain to recall why he had awakened from an unnatural sleep to this level of discomfort that had triggered hallucinations. For as soon as he realised he was not in imminent danger of being burned to a cinder he had total recall of all that had happened between the time he found Rosebud Petrie and her baby and when the booted foot of Stan Tait was launched toward his face.

Now he recognised that it was early morning: that the flames of the fire burned in competition with the greyness of the pre-dawn light rather than the glow of the moon. Next saw that the man who lived in the house on the promontory of rock was no longer garbed in work clothes. Instead wore a dark-hued outfit of a Stetson, shirt with a kerchief at the open neck, vest, jacket and pants that did not comprise a suit, spurred riding boots and a double-holstered gunbelt. In the holsters were the matched pair of Remingtons Steele had seen mounted on the wall above the fireplace in the Murchisons' parlour.

He saw this as the man rose from the chair and came toward him, rifle in one hand and cup of coffee in the other. The cup was set down on the ground and then Murchison returned to the chair, his leather-textured and life-wearied face as empty of feeling as his tone of voice had been. And while this act of undemonstrative giving was completed, Steele took in other components of his present circumstances.

Recognised that Murchison had appropriated one of the chairs from the wagon while he waited for its owner to regain consciousness. But not before he had made Steele a little more comfortable—improvised a pillow for his punished head and covered him with blankets and the sheepskin coat without moving him from where he had fallen. When he realised this, he rolled his head too quickly to look to where he had first bedded down beneath the wagon: then had to wait for the blinding level of pain to subside before the area of flattened grass came into focus.

'Wasn't them that tucked you up all cosy like,' Clay Murchison said. 'It was me found that beat-up old rifle Abe Lincoln give you, Steele. It's safe on your wagon.'

He rolled his head more gingerly. Saw the cup in sharp outline and had just a blurred impression of the man on the chair in the far background. For the first time became aware of the smell of the coffee and chose to concentrate on this: relishing how a hot drink would wash the sand out of his throat as he struggled to fold up into a seated attitude. When he achieved this, he swung his legs out from under the covers and rested his back to a wheel of the hay wagon.

He knew he must have fallen well after Parker hit him with the revolver. And the jerking action of his body when Tait kicked him had done no serious damage. For all the pain was in his head. And this was easier to take now, after it became concentrated at the two points of violent impact.

The coffee did not taste as good as it smelled until he had taken several sips. Then he sighed in satisfaction and chanced to speak. Told his benefactor:

'I'm grateful to you, Murchison.'

'Thanks ain't what I done any of it for, Steele. Help's what I'm seekin'.'

Dawn was fully broken. A bunch of birds in the surrounding pine forests began to call conflicting announcements of the new day. The chorus drowned out the distant gurgling of the stream down in the valley. Horses snorted.

And Steele did a double take at the animals. Saw that one of the team geldings was missing. The strange horse was another gelding, but he was a strawberry roan.

Murchison saw the way the Virginian glanced away from the animals and then took a second, harder look. Said: 'That one's mine. They stole one of your team. For my wife to ride, I figure. I ain't got no way of knowin' what else they took of your property, Steele. I'm still pretty damn good at readin' sign, but there's limits. Just know that my wife was stole. Bare ass naked, exceptin' for her coat.'

Murchison's eyes, which were light blue in bloodshot surrounds, cracked to narrow slits in the first brightness of the rising sun. And Steele found himself compelled to look at the same spot on the ground upon which they were fixed—saw the improvised pillow was made up of the once elegant ball gown, folded several times.

'What she was wearin' underneath is balled up inside it,' the man went on, and the strain of sustaining an outward show of cool composure was just discernible as a faint crack in his otherwise still even-toned voice. 'I ain't much for tendin' sick people, but I done what seemed to be right, Steele.'

There was an implied apology in the conclusion of the

66

brief explanation. And for awhile Steele's physical pain was dispelled by a sense of shame. This as he vividly recalled how he ignored his good intentions to refuse the offer made by Chrissy Murchison and then surrendered to the temptation to take her available body. And now the woman's husband was on the defensive to him . . .

But suddenly the pains in his head swamped the pangs of conscience: as the memory of his lust was displaced by an even clearer mental image—of the bruises that marred the beauty of Chrissy's face. Bruises raised by the violent fists of a wife beater and a bigot who had refused to give aid to a tiny black baby and yet now sought help for——

'Zachery, Goddamnit!' Steele snarled. And tossed aside the cup, splashing coffee over the once fine dress. This as he twisted and hooked both gloved hands to wheel spokes. Then grimaced against an urge to give vent to sharper pains as he hauled himself upright.

'They didn't take the baby, Steele,' Murchison said dully. And his voice seemed to come from a long way off. 'I found him just like you see him.'

Steele could not see Zachery Petrie. Not for three more seconds or so. And as he heard what the man said, but learned nothing from the tone, his tormented mind conjured up an image of the awesome wound that had killed Rosebud Petrie. While he fought with all his willpower to blank out a picture of the baby, blood splattered and utterly still.

Such an awesome figment of imagination did appear, but it never came into sharp focus. And then it was banished to the limbo of proven futile concerns, when Steele reached a position from which he could look into the hope chest become a crib shaded from the early morning sun by a blanket. Where the infant slept peacefully: still warmly covered from the chill of the night by a caring woman who had been allowed to scrawl a message on a piece of paper torn from a book. It lay on the blanket draped form: *Zacherys bin change and feed some. I hopes.* Obviously the impatience of the three men to leave the night camp had prevented Chrissy from finishing her message.

'That's something,' Steele rasped breathlessly as he turned away from the wagon but stayed on his feet. Leaned against the wheel, feeling drained in mind and body.

'I ain't no hypocrite, Steele,' Clay Murchison said as he rose to his feet. Began to kick at the fire to put out the flames. 'So I ain't gonna make out I give much of a damn about that Negro kid.'

The Virginian slowly shook his head and eyed the man with acrimony as he replied: 'That's something else, feller.'

'Person can't help how he feels,' Murchison countered tonelessly. 'What he can do is be true to his feelin's. And everyone that knows me allows that I'm that all right.'

Steele now noticed something about the man who had become old before his time that had failed to register when he brought the coffee across from the fire. The Virginian had been too preoccupied indulging his own discomforts to see that Murchison was in as much or maybe even greater pain. This affected his limbs—arms and legs alike—and caused him to make each move with considerable care. While Steele watched him douse the fire he recalled their first meeting beside the house on the outcrop of rock. When he had assumed Murchison's stiff jointed gait was caused by the aching joints of a long day's manual work. Back then the sudden appearance of a stranger on his place had alarmed him and a volatile mixture of fear and hostility had transcended pain when he hurried toward the house. Here at the start of a bright new day the man moved with a practised deliberateness:

made an expert over a long time in how best to do what must be done with the least amount of discomfort from diseased joints.

'Love that woman you were takin' away from me, Steele. More than anythin' else in the world. Might not sound like the truth to you, but truth it is. Intend to bring her back to the place.' His head was bowed as he made the pronouncement, watching what he was doing as he trod out the final glowing embers. Then he looked up and turned around to gaze fixedly at the Virginian, a tacit question in his deep-set eyes.

Steele said: 'I'll need to put your horse in the traces?'

'The animal's as used to pullin' a wagon as to bein' saddle rode. I'm obliged you're goin' to help me.' He advanced on the Virginian, switching the Winchester to his left hand so he could extend his right. 'Whatever scores there are between us are forgotten?'

The handshake was brief, by mutal consent. Both were impassive-faced, until Steele said as Murchison stowed his rifle under the seat:

'You've got no unsettled scores with me, feller. I wasn't taking your wife away from you.'

Murchison had been about to go bring the horses. He halted, his back toward Steele. More rigid in his stance than was necessary to ease the rheumatic pains. Probably needing to make a considerable effort to quell an impulse to anger, Steele thought. Then, weariness in his tone, the older man replied:

'I accept what you say, Steele. And if there's anythin' else to be said about anythin', best it's done while we're rollin'?'

Only then did he turn his head so that Steele could see his face that showed just a trace of a scowl. And a nod of agreement by the younger man acted to erase this final sign of high, hostile emotion. Then, true to their pact, there were no further exchanges between them while the preparations to leave were completed: Murchison attending to the harnessing of the horses while Steele re-stacked the freight that he had moved to give the woman a sleeping space. The Virginian also loaded the chair Murchison had taken off the wagon, and the man's saddle and gear. He did not touch the red gown rolled up around Chrissy's underthings. Murchison did, tossing the bundle into the wagon before he climbed cautiously up and sat down beside Steele. Then sighed as the only discernible sign of his hurting. Before he suggested:

'Figure they'll have headed for Providence. That's down into the valley and follow the creek.'

Steele set the wagon rolling in the direction Murchison pointed out. And acknowledged to himself that he was feeling a whole lot better as far as the pain of his swollen jaw and that at the side of his head were concerned. For these discomforts had diminished to an extent that left him aware of the thick growth of bristles on his lower face and the feel—and smell—of yesterday's sweat and travel dust that was still on his flesh. Probably, he allowed, he was more pointedly conscious of his unwashed and unshaven state because Clay Murchison was so relatively neatly turned out this morning.

'The sign showed they started off on the way to town,' the again impassive-faced man went on in his customary monotone as the wagon began the descent into the valley. 'But even if there wasn't no sign, Providence is a safe bet. Got money in the bank there. The girl would need money. She's allowed to make withdrawals. Trusted her far as that went. Money, I mean.'

The water of the twenty-feet-wide stream looked cool and refreshing with the sunlight glinting on it. Up close it was seen to be crystal clear as polished glass, shallow enough for the pebble-strewn bed to show up beneath the gently moving surface. The higher volume of the gurgling sounds at close quarters added to the compelling invitation. And as soon as the wagon was alongside the stream bank, Steele hauled on the reins to bring the rig to a halt. The strawberry roan and the grey complied with the command, but not until they had turned across the gravel bank and reached a point where they could dip their heads to drink.

'Here,' Steele said, and thrust the reins towards Murchison. Then made to swing down off the seat.

The older man took the reins automatically while his thoughts were elsewhere. But a moment later he demanded: 'What's wrong?'

'Me, feller. Feeling better but starting to smell bad.'

'I can live with that!' Murchison snarled, and with his free hand drew one of the matched Remingtons. Thumbed back the hammer as part of the smooth action of sliding the revolver from the holster: so that it was ready to fire the moment the muzzle drew a bead on Steele. Was aimed at the Virginian's suddenly frowning face, for he was standing on a wheel spoke and almost down off the wagon before the other man was startled into making the menacing response. 'You can get cleaned up in town.'

He had moderated his tone now and an expression of apprehension spread across his deeply-lined face as he began to regret the impulsive action. And his discomfiture increased as the Virginian told him:

'Whatever you say.'

He spoke the words of submission in an even tone. And there was an expression of nonchalant acceptance of the inevitable on his face in the wake of a look that had been caught midway between a frown of shock and a scowl of fear.

'I'm sorry, but I figure we oughta make as good time as we can to——' He had started to push the Remington back in the holster as he spoke the apology with total sincerity. Abruptly reversed the move. Sought to aim the Remington at Steele again as the Virginian switched from

71

resignation to malevolence. But Murchison was too late: perhaps because his reflexes were slowed by the surge of pain caused by the abrupt speed of the first draw. Then, part of a second later, he was engulfed by a greater agony that forced a shrill cry from between his gritted teeth. This as he was jerked violently sideways, his legs flying upwards and his shoulder crashing to the seat. Wrenched into such an attitude by Steele's left hand as the right whipped up and forward to threaten the agonised and terrified man with the knife drawn from the boot sheath.

'I've had enough, you wife-beating, negro-hating son-ofabitch!' the Virginian rasped against a burst of wailing from Zachery Petrie awakened by Murchison's cry. 'You listen to me and you listen hard! Okay?'

He stood firmly on a wheel spoke, his position secured by a tight grip on the coat collar of the other man. Murchison breathed raggedly but was otherwise unmoving with his eyes pushed to the far limits of their sockets to fasten his attention on the knife: the point of which was less than an inch above his cheek.

'I asked you okay!' Steele snarled. And twisted his grip on the coat collar, at the same time as he carefully lowered the knife so that the point rested on the age-toughened skin of the face but did not puncture it.

Murchison swallowed hard and opened his mouth to respond. But only a dry gagging sound emerged. And then he shifted the direction of his gaze: to peer into the compassionless features of the man who threatened him. On his face, in back of the terror, was a tacit plea for understanding his constricted throat did not allow him to speak.

The baby continued to howl and just for a moment Steele allowed his attention to be drawn toward Zachery. And, released from the power of the Virginian's demanding eyes, Murchison was able to rasp:

'Yeah . . . Okay . . . I know I was outta line to——'

Steele turned his hand holding the coat collar still more. And altered the position of the knife. To rest the flat of the sun-glinting blade across the hollow cheek. Said evenly: 'I'm looking to get out of this business, feller. I reckoned I was out of it until I found a dying mother and her baby. Because I want to be out of this business I had to bring the kid with me. And I couldn't leave him at the house of a bigot like you. I had to make a deal with your wife: a ride into town in exchange for her taking care of the baby. Then those three hard men showed up. And if it hadn't been for your wife I'd be too damn dead to be concerned with how I smell. That puts me back in this business, Murchison!'

His voice became an ill-tempered snarl as he rounded off the monologue. When the man sprawled along the seat began to blurt:

'I don't know what . . . What business you talkin' about, Steele? I ain't . . . I told you I was——'

'The death business,' Steele cut in on the man whose fear-filled voice was barely discernible against the increasingly strident cries of the baby. 'And I reckon you know by now you came damn close to being my first customer this time around?'

'I acted crazy, Steele! I know it. But I'm so worried sick about——'

'Take the cure,' the Virginian drawled as he let go his hold on Murchison's coat and withdrew the knife. Dropped to the ground and added: 'You almost worried yourself to death.'

7

Clay Murchison said dully: 'I was a lawman for the Union Pacific before I got shot up bad. That was up in San Francisco after I tracked a bunch of train robbers to a warehouse on the waterfront.'

The hay wagon was rolling again. The older man held the reins now, while Steele had Zachery Petrie cradled in one arm. Feeding the contented baby with milk transferred from the tin cup to the tiny mouth with the fingers of his free hand. A hand that was a good deal cleaner than it had been when the Virginian developed this method of feeding the night before.

Not just his hands and face had felt the benefit of the cool water worked into a soapy lather before he shaved off almost twenty-four hours of tough bristles—needing to use the razor gingerly on the swollen area of his jawline. For he had taken the opportunity to strip to the waist and wash off the old sweat from his torso.

Zachery had cried constantly while Steele indulged himself in the luxury of washing up and shaving. And Clay Murchison gradually regained his composure while he sat rigidly erect on the wagon seat: the fear and pain of the recent eruption of violence making him deaf to the shrill howling for a long time. Then, maybe, the ear-piercing barrage of wails acted to underpin the man's diminishing resentment toward everyone responsible for his present circumstances.

The Virginian took no longer than was needed to do what he felt was necessary: remained aware of the crying baby and the rancorous man but did not allow either the noise or the acrimonious glances to trouble him. And it was coincidental that when he climbed back aboard the wagon his impassive face was a true reflection of how he felt. For he had not consciously used the time at the stream bank to ease himself free of anger.

There had been no talk as Steele began the preparations to feed the baby. Just an exchange of glances when Murchison asked permission to start the wagon—gestured with the reins—and drew a nod of agreement. And they had been rolling for more than a half mile, the baby making only quiet sucking sounds on the milky fingers, when Murchison broke his long silence.

Steele replied: 'Reckon it was a good time, before that. Way you had the badge and revolvers hung on the wall at your house?'

He spoke evenly. Holding up one end of a conversation while he fed Zachery automatically and was able to maintain his customary watch over the surrounding country.

'The best. I was good at what I did with the railroad company. But I knew I was gettin' close to the finish. Started to get the rheumatism aches in all my joints. Managed to keep it to myself for a time. But people began to notice. Way I moved. Way sometimes I couldn't keep from showin' it hurt when I moved the wrong way.'

He glanced at Steele and mistook the reason for the younger man's seeming disinterest in what he was telling him. Said sourly: 'I ain't just talkin' to make a noise, Steele. But if you'd rather I stay quiet while you admire the scenery, then——'

'I'm listening, feller. Last night I almost got killed by paying too much attention to——'

'Okay, I get the point. But it won't be the men that

75

jumped you last night . . . If anyone sharpshoots at us from up in the trees. Sign shows them still headin' for Providence.'

The Virginian had seen this for himself. The grass grew long and green and tender on the valley bottom at either side of the clear, slow-running stream. In the early morning sunlight that cast elongated shadows it could be clearly seen where several horses had trampled the turf ahead of the wagon. In back of the rig were the deep ruts made by its wheels.

'It's the only sign to be seen, feller,' Steele said.

'Regular trail's up in the timber beyond the ridge.' He jerked a thumb to indicate the top of the valley's eastern flank. 'I don't even know if you can get a wagon into town from this way.'

Zachery let it be known with a pushing action of his tongue that he had had his fill of milk. Then he smiled his consent to being replaced in the hope chest under the shade blanket. Steele thought Murchison was as relieved as he was when the baby made no wailing protest at being back in the improvised crib.

'Anyway, like I was tellin' you, Steele. A couple of bullets in the back and another one in the belly as I turned settled my hash with the railroad. But the company showed their appreciation. Give me a chunk of cash when I was healed from the bullet wounds. On top of payin' all the doctorin' bills. Enough for me to come down to this piece of country and build the house on the rock. Saw it a long time ago, that rock. When I chased a couple of hold-up men down here. Decided right there and then . . . If I lived long enough to retire, that's where I'd retire to. Back then, I didn't have no young wife.'

Steele was aware of the surreptitious sidelong glance directed at him as Murchison made this first mention of Chrissy. And he supplied the prompt that seemed to be requested of him. 'She didn't take to it?'

'She would've,' the older man answered morosely. And peered intently ahead, but probably was not looking at where the valley narrowed and curved to the left between less high sides: lower, but much steeper, with timber on the ridges still and just an occasional thicket of brush clinging to the sides of what was becoming a ravine. The stream was running faster now: deeper and noisier. Zachery sometimes laughed at the splashing sounds. Clay Murchison expressed something very close to a smile as he examined a piece of the past. 'See, she wasn't a city girl. Was born and raised on a farm in the Dakotas. Her folks were killed in a Sioux uprisin' and she took to runnin' with a kid who fell in with some bad company and went bad himself.'

He sent a globule of saliva off the side of the wagon and seemed only now to realise how dramatically the terrain had changed. That soon there would be no grassy banks to the stream as it plunged between sheer walls of limestone twenty feet apart and twice this high. The pebbled bed of the watercourse was still visible, no more than three feet below the fast-flowing surface, and the ravine was still just as wide where it curved to the right and out of sight.

'What d'you figure, Steele?' the older man asked nervously, and made to haul on the reins.

The Virginian reached across and took the reins from Murchison, who was obviously happy to surrender them. And the wagon continued to move at the same easy pace as before. Steele said:

'Your wife figured just a couple of miles or so from where I made night camp to town?'

'About that,' Murchison confirmed, still anxious. 'As the crow flies. But we never did come this way. Always took the trail to town.'

They had run out of dry land and the two horses in the traces submitted to being steered into the stream without any sign of shying. In the chest under the blanket, the baby began to laugh more heartily at the higher volume of splashing sounds and the rougher ride as hooves and wheels plunged through water over pebbles.

'Reckon this is where Providence gets its water?' Steele asked, needing to raise his voice to be heard.

Murchison nodded, then warned: 'But ain't no tellin' how narrow and deep it gets before it reaches town.'

Steele displayed a brief grin that drew back his lips but failed to inject humour into his coal-black eyes as he countered: 'A man can't be in the death business without taking chances, feller.'

The older man scowled at a recent memory. Then took a firm grip on the seat at either side and grimaced with present pain as the juddering of the wagon jarred his diseased joints. But within a few moments he was able to express a smile that showed far more pleasure than that which had fleetingly altered the set of Steele's face. This as the wagon rounded the turn in water up to its wheelhubs and the men saw a broad expanse of open country ahead. A vista that quickly opened out wider as the ravine walls splayed apart and lost height with every yard.

'Providence is over there beyond them trees where the creek's headed,' Murchison announced, and the same brand of relief displayed on his gaunt face now sounded in his tone. 'I guess you can see the smoke, uh?'

The stream stretched in two long curves toward one of many stands of timber scattered over a vast area of rich, gently rolling land with dark, high mountain ranges on the distant horizons to the north, east and west. A trail that came down off the high ground through which the valley and the ravine cut could also be seen to disappear into the same clump of trees a half mile to the north east. Above the timber, a pall of dark woodsmoke gathered from many stove fires stained the clear morning air.

Elsewhere, other traces of smoke could be seen. In some cases the farmhouses from which the smoke rose were visibly out in the open: in others the buildings were hidden by trees. Here and there a run of fencing showed against the lush grass of meadows. And some strips of red dirt trails that linked the scattered places with the road to the town in the timber.

'Yeah, Chrissy loves this piece of California, Steele,' Murchison took up his recollections again as the wagon came out of the water and on to grassland and the ride became smoother and quieter. And Zachery Petrie began to gurgle in unknowing imitation of the smooth running stream. 'This country around town, and way out in the back of beyond where we built the house and are clearin' a space in the trees to raise crops. Says it reminds her of the Dakotas where she grew up. Except that the weather's a whole lot better in these parts.'

After his voice trailed away on a sorrowful note, he once more spat to the side. And the final traces of the smile drained off his haggard face. And then his tone became abruptly embittered when he switched the period of his delving into the past to explain: 'That's not so long ago, course. No, when I first came across Chrissy she didn't have no good feelin's for nothin'.' He swallowed hard and spat again. Growled: 'Hell, sure wish I'd brought a bottle with me!'

Steele looked hard at Clay Murchison for the first time since he had trapped the man to the wagon seat with the threat of the knife. And saw how much older he had seemed to grow since then. He was sweating, too. And blinking his eyes a lot. Dry-washed his hands where they lay on his bony thighs. And the Virginian thought a brand of pain unrelated to the man's rheumatism was causing all these visible signs: that right now he was a drunk in dire need of a drink. Or maybe, he corrected himself, the aches in the punished joints had started to trouble him worse than before. Perhaps the dulling effect of hard liquor was sometimes all that made the agony bearable?

'She belonged to the whole bunch by then,' Murchison made haste to continue, like he was intent upon using talk to keep his mind off the need for a drink. 'He was a weak-willed little runt, that kid that took her away after she was made an orphan. She was thirteen when it happened with the Indians. And he was maybe two years older. The bad company they finished up with were mostly full grown men. The kid just couldn't keep them from havin' their share of her.

'Then I led the posse that trapped the whole bunch of them in their hide-out up in Oregon. After they'd hit one of our trains and killed some people. We killed four of them sonsofbitches and saw to it the other three won't never come outta the penitentiary until it's in boxes. Chrissy was the only woman . . . girl. Her I took care of. Had her to live with my sister Hortense in San Francisco and saw to it she didn't want for nothin' to keep herself decent until time did some healin' of what she'd suffered since losin' her folks. Suffered in the mind more than the body, seems to me?'

He came from out of the past to look at Steele and his deep-set eyes altered the opinion into a request for agreement. This as the Virginian completed his assessment of the rolling countryside through which they were moving—angling away from the stream now because at least two barbed wire property fences blocked that way into town. So he was steering the wagon toward the trail.

'I can see how that was likely to be so,' he allowed after he had concluded a piece of country such as this would have suited his purpose perfectly: before it was settled by others.

Again Murchison was irritated by the detachment of Adam Steele. But he confined his reaction to the apparent indifference to a scowl as he looked away from the man at his side. And hurried on once more, eager to get to his point before his audience of one lost interest entirely.

'Upshot of it was, Chrissy and me got hitched soon as she was feelin' well again. It was pretty much of a spring and fall match, I guess. But she surely wanted to marry me. And me . . . Well, you seen what a fine lookin' young woman she turned into? That was two years ago come the seventh of next month. But three weeks after we got wed, I was shot up in the warehouse trouble. And it was more than three months before I was over the worst of it. Or it seemed like the worst of it, anyways.'

They reached the trail and turned on to it, the hooves and wheels churning up fine red dust. The baby had started to whimper and a bad smell wafting up from out of the chest under the blanket sunshade provided an obvious clue to the reason for Zachery's fractiousness. But then he quietened, and with their journey's end almost in sight, Steele decided he could live with the ripe odour until they reached Providence.

'We decided right off to leave Frisco,' Murchison said. 'Soon as it was plain I wasn't no more use to the railroad company and they gave me the big pay off. Chrissy was all for it. She'd heard me talkin' often enough about the place in the valley I'd picked out for a house. And the doc who took care of me, he said it should be fine. Help heal me from being shot. And maybe keep my joints from stiffenin' up so bad: if I took it a little easy on the buildin' chores.'

Murchison sent a stream of saliva through the rising dust and growled sourly: 'Boy, was that sawbones wrong. About the rheumatics that ain't never stopped hurtin' worse than ever before since I did the first day's work on the house. Though I guess I can't hold it against the doc for what happened about the slug I took in the belly. Low down . . . If you get my drift?'

He directed another sidelong glance at Steele, and chewed on his lower lip. And the Virginian asked:

'You trying to work around to tell me you couldn't be a real husband to your wife, feller?'

Murchison blew some air through pursed lips and rubbed a coat sleeve back and forth on his brow to wipe away the beads of sweat. 'Damn it, could I use a drink . . . Yeah, that's right, Steele. Not after the shoot out at the warehouse. Way I was so sick in Frisco, I wasn't in no fit state to be concerned with that kinda thing. It didn't show up until me and Chrissy got down to the valley. See, I still got what it takes . . . On the outside. Still got me a pecker and balls. But I ain't got what it takes inside no more. Since that lead drilled into my belly. Impotence is what it's called.'

Steele nodded. 'Yeah, I know that, feller. That's real rough. On the both of you.'

There was a note of genuine sympathy in his voice, but his face remained impassive as he caught his first glimpse of the town that came into view among the trees. This was a small clapboard church with a short spire, painted white. At the side of the church was a cemetery enclosed by a low fieldstone wall. Two men were digging in a corner of the cemetery.

'Ain't no argument with that, Steele. But it wasn't so bad between Chrissy and me. Not at first, when I found out I couldn't screw no more. She said it didn't matter. Reckoned she'd had enough of that kinda thing to last her two lifetimes when she was being shared around by that bunch of outlaws. And maybe it was the truth. The honest to God truth!'

He was peering at the church now. And the other buildings that came into partial view beyond it. But bitterness that threatened to trigger an outburst of anger had spread a hard set scowl across his face. And it was apparent, once again, that ugly images from the past obscured the peaceful scene of sunlit and shade dappled pastoral beauty at which he gazed with such a fixed stare. Then, after it had taken him a few seconds to control the swell of rage, he went on: 'There's a good chance it was all my fault. After I took to drinkin' so much. After the ache of wantin' her got to be worse than the rheumatics, Steele. After workin' on the place from sun up to sundown didn't do nothin' to kill the wantin' of her. Good chance, shit! It was my fault. It was me got drunk. Me who called her a lyin' bitch and worst for tellin' me it didn't matter to her . . . That I couldn't give her what a woman needs from a man. It was me started in to beat up on her when callin' her names wasn't enough no more. And whenever I figured Chrissy was lookin' at men . . Thinkin' how it could be . . .'

He dragged a coat sleeve across his face again, and maybe it was just beads of sweat he wiped off his flesh, Steele allowed. Then Murchison vented a short sigh that sounded of resignation. And the crack in his voice had been repaired when he concluded the admission of guilt:

'Hell, mister, the wonder of it is that Chrissy didn't run off from me before. The way I treated her so bad?'

Once more the expressing of an opinion was transformed into a request. Both in his tone of voice and the abruptly helpless look in his eyes as he switched his attention from the past to Steele.

'Sure sounds like it,' the Virginian said, as disinterested as he appeared to be while he surveyed the town of Providence. And experienced a sense of bitter-sweet nostalgia because the place reminded him so strongly of any one of a number of small communities that had been features of the Virginia countryside in which he had grown up. But even if memories of his own past had not intruded on the recollections Clay Murchison was relating, Steele was sure his attitude to the man would have been much the same. For the facts had been stated. The man had been offered as much sympathy as he was going to get on account of his impotence. Now Murchison was seeking to justify his drunken violence toward his wife, and fishing for Steele to salve his conscience with comforting words that condoned his actions. But the Virginian went no further than the flatly-spoken agreement.

And then, as Murchison shifted his doleful gaze to watch the two men digging a grave in the cemetery as the wagon rolled past, he asked in the manner of someone who does not expect to receive a response: 'Did you and my Chrissy get to screwin' last night, Steele?'

'No, feller,' the Virginian replied. And memories of the far more recent past displaced those of his childhood and youth. Memories that triggered a brand of guilt that he was sure must have sounded in his voice when he gave the fast answer.

After a pause of several seconds, Murchison allowed: 'I believe you.'

This as both he and Steele saw the grave-diggers do a double-take toward the wagon. Before the coveralled, hatless men returned to their chore with a haste and will that had not been apparent before. Like they were embarrassed to have been caught staring at the rig and now attempted to pretend a total lack of interest in it.

And Steele felt suddenly angry that he had let guilt influence his attitude toward this drunken bigot of a wife-beater. Said, close to a snarl: 'I don't give a damn what you believe, feller.'

'Guess you don't,' Murchison replied without rancour. Then sighed before he added: 'I don't know if I oughta feel better or worse about that. You and her not screwin', I mean. On account of it kinda makes me think it was true what Chrissy told me so many times. About her havin' had her fill of men that way. Ain't no denyin' you have to look a whole lot better to a woman than a used-up old-timer like me, Steele. And if Chrissy had felt the need bad, she surely would've let you know she was ready and willin' to——'

'She did,' Steele cut in, and acknowledged to himself that he was probably unjustified in getting piqued at

84

Murchison for stirring up the disconcerting feeling of guilt.

The pause left by the older man this time was much longer and his expression was akin to a grimace when he at last blurted incredulously: 'And you didn't want a woman as fine lookin' as Chrissy?' He looked set to explode with anger as he prepared to accuse Steele of lying to him earlier. But then he thought of something else and bit back on this approach so that he could demand in a scornful tone: 'Or maybe you don't like women so much, eh? I call to mind I heard tales about some dudes that ain't so keen on women. Like to go with——'

'I'm not that kind,' Steele broke in evenly. And appeared to survey his surroundings with a greater intensity of concentration while he struggled to control a fresh urge to anger.

'So how come you and her didn't get to——'

'I told you,' the Virginian said, aware of the accusing stare that Murchison directed at his impassive profile. 'Three other men came between us.'

Now Clay Murchison groaned and Steele met his gaze, as the contempt disappeared from the deep-set, bloodshot eyes and was replaced with the same degree of misery that had sounded in the low-pitched exclamation. And it was clear the man had temporarily forgotten about the late night intruders on the night camp.

'So you figure you would've . . ? With her . . ? If those guys hadn't showed up and . . ?'

'Can't deny it.'

'Hell, I'm sorry, Steele. For sayin' I thought you was a——'

'Forget it, feller. No apologies are necessary from either of us, I reckon. Whichever way you look at it, it was a fruitless night.'

85

8

Adam Steele quickly revised his first impression of Providence as a town like many he had seen in his younger days in a state on the far side of the country from this California community.

It was the white-painted clapboard church and the other timber-construction buildings beside the church and across the street from it which had sparked his nostalgia. These were a half dozen houses, one and two storied, which were also white painted. Set back from the unside-walked dirt street behind fenced gardens. Beyond this strip of straight street that cut into the southern fringe of the trees, Providence seemed to be not so much a town as a number of relatively isolated buildings erected on sites scattered throughout the stand of timber. The street sometimes seemed to revert to a trail as it meandered among the pines and live oaks, birches and maples, spruces and willows: when no buildings were in sight and just spurs at either side indicated there were places far back in the timber. Houses probably, like those that could be seen from the slow-rolling wagon. These mostly of a single story, built of various materials that ranged from simple split logs to bricks of red or yellow or grey. Some of them as well maintained in neatly tended gardens as those in the area of the church. Others rundown, standing directly at the side of the trail-like street, or a few set back behind hard-packed front yards or weed-choked plots that had maybe started out as gardens.

Smoke curled up from every visible chimney, rising toward a sky that was in large part obscured by the timber: the fragrances of woodsmoke and cooking food almost masking the unsavoury aroma that emanated from the baby in the makeshift crib. Apart from the pair of men in the cemetery who had attempted to conceal their keen interest in the passing hay wagon, the smoke from the house chimneys was the only sign of life to be seen in Providence. Until a small girl of six or seven appeared at the open doorway of a stone and timber house to gaze at the early morning passersby with the guileless frankness of childhood. A few moments later, obviously drawn to take a look outside the house by the sounds of the wagon's progress, a middle-aged woman stepped into the doorway at the side of the child. She stared hard for a stretched second, then jerked the girl backwards and slammed the door closed with a crash that put a flock of birds to startled flight.

'That ain't got nothin' to do with you, Steele,' Clay Murchison murmured. 'Same as with those two that was doin' the grave-diggin' back there. It's on account of me. I'm about as welcome in Providence as a fox in a chicken coop.'

The Virginian nodded, mildly satisfied that his instinct for recognising unseen hostility that had failed him during a time of lust was proved to be functioning now that he was riding a killing trail once more. He said evenly: 'Between the fellers at the cemetery and that woman, a whole bunch of others looked at this rig and wished they weren't seeing what they saw.'

The older man spat off the side of the wagon. 'You knew we was being watched from behind windows we couldn't see into, eh? Yeah, it figures a man like you'd be able to spot that kinda thing, Steele. I was real mixed up when I said I thought you was the kind of fancy threaded dude that went for——' Another spit, as the wagon came out of a series of sharp bends with no buildings or spurs on either side and a brightly sunlit town square opened up directly ahead. 'Way you been since you came outta being unconscious . . . Everythin' you done . . . Almost everythin' you said . . . Most all of it goes against you being the kind that I accused you of being. And against the kind that drives a wagon load of household chattels around the country. And with a baby in the back, as well. Damn it, Steele . . . In the kinda spot I'm in now, I figure you're just the kinda man I need to help me. I said that once already, didn't I? Back at where I found you?'

'That's right,' the Virginian replied, detached again after most of his attention had shifted away from the man at his side. 'And like I told you, Murchison—or if I didn't, I should have. Whatever I do to catch up with Parker and his two sidekicks, and what I do to them when I locate them . . . That doesn't have anything to do with me wanting to help you.'

'Look, I——' Murchison started, and even in these two syllables there was a distinct tone of ingratiation. Before he responded to the abruptness of how Steele reined in the team. Then the older man snapped his head around to peer in the same direction as the Virginian.

This as a man ordered in grim tones:

'Set the brake lever, stranger. Then reach. Murchison, you unbuckle the gunbelt and toss it off the wagon. Then you reach.'

There were just trees flanking the end of the trail-like street on the south side of the square. On the western side was a line of stores, timber built and sharing a continuous stretch of roofed sidewalk two steps up from the ground level. Facing the stores across some five hundred feet of hard-packed red dirt was a mixture of brick, stone and timber constructed buildings, each separated from its neighbour by a wagon-wide alley. A stage line depot, a bank, a livery stable and a boarding house. At the centre of the northern side, immediately opposite the point where the street from the south entered the symmetrically planned square, was the start of another street—or maybe it at once became the open trail. To the left of this from the viewpoint of the men aboard the wagon halted some halfway across the square was a meeting hall and a schoolhouse. To the right was the law office, a newspaper printing plant and a saloon. The boarding house was the only two storied building on the square and like the meeting hall, school and saloon it was of frame construction. The law office was built of grey stone, maybe granite.

Until Steele saw the door of the law office swing open, the only signs of life on the large square were the seven horses hitched to a rail out front of Grout's Livery Stable. All the animals saddled, looking fresh and rested and eager to wear down shoe iron. Then, after the one man stepped out across the law office threshold and began to issue the orders, six others emerged from the same doorway between a large curtained window and a much smaller one that was barred. Three moved to the left and three to the right. Then all seven halted in a tense line. Just the first man out aimed a rifle from his shoulder. The others thrust revolvers to the limit of their reach at the men on the wagon seat.

'What the hell you doin', Fallows?' Murchison countered. He tried to sound authoritative but there was a huskiness of fear in his tone. 'And the rest of you men? My wife's been——'

'We know better than you what happened to Mrs Murchison!' a man at the end of the line broke in, his voice scathing. This as an eighth man showed himself in the law office doorway but did not come through it. From his coveralls and the way he breathed so heavily, it was clear he was one of the early morning grave-diggers: who had needed to run from one side of the town to the other to get there ahead of the wagon. 'Do like the sheriff tells you. Like the stranger's done.'

Steele had wasted no time in complying with the orders of the tall, lean, black-moustached man of fifty or so who aimed the Winchester at a constant height as he tracked it slowly from side to side over a short arc: drawing a bead by turns on both men on the wagon seat.

'What's happened to Chrissy?' Murchison snapped. And this time it was fear for his wife rather than of the men with levelled guns that cracked his voice. 'She left the house and then——'

'Sooner you do like you been told, sooner you'll know,' the most nervous-looking man in the line replied quickly.

Murchison raked his confused gaze from what looked to be a ready-to-ride posse to direct a tacit plea for explanation to the Virginian who continued to hold the stoic, arms raised attitude. But then Steele started to rasp out of the side of his mouth:

'Do like they tell you and I reckon we'll find out——'

Fallows' rifle exploded a shot. The report was far more shockingly obtrusive on the peace of the sunlit morning than any of the raised voices had been. The bullet streaked high—far above the heads of the men on the seat of the hay wagon. But within a second the spent cartridge case had been ejected, a fresh shell was in the breech and the barrel was making its threatening swing back and forth between Steele and Murchison again.

'Me and the men have got some ridin' to do,' the Providence sheriff said flatly. 'The sooner——'

He cut himself short when he heard Zachery Petrie vent a howl of delayed protest to the sound of the gunshot.

'A baby!' the nervous man gasped. 'They've got a baby!'

Some of the revolver-toting men took a few paces forward, rasping their surprise. Until Fallows snarled:

'Shut up and stay where you are!' Then he waited for the order to be obeyed and for the howls to subside to a whimper before he checked the raking movement of the rifle. And trained the muzzle in a rock steady aim at Murchison. Warned: 'Do like I told you or you'll have another bullet wound to gripe about. If you live to gripe about it. I mean it. We never had this kind of trouble in town before.'

'I just don't get this, I don't get it at all,' Murchison said in confusion and swung his gaze between the Providence sheriff and Steele. But as he complained of his non-comprehension his bony fingers fumbled with the buckle of his gunbelt. And when it came loose he tossed it off the wagon to the right.

'Now get down from there,' Fallows instructed with less force. Gestured with the rifle. 'Both to that side.'

All the seven men who had emerged from the law office had been tense until the gunbelt with the twin holsters hit the square. Now they began to feel easier by stages: and only the sheriff remained taut and a hairsbreadth from squeezing the Winchester trigger again after Steele and Murchison were down off the wagon. This seen clearly on his sun-burnished and rough-hewn face that was no longer partially obscured by the rifle which he now aimed from the waist.

'Len, shall I go bring a woman to take care of the baby?' the short and skinny nervous man suggested.

'One that doesn't care he's black,' Steele drawled.

There was a babble of talk among the men. And the Virginian was certain he heard the name *Petrie* spoken several times. Before Fallows ended the perplexed exchanges with:

'Yeah, Dan. Bring Arlene Forrester if she's up to it.'

The man who had volunteered for the errand looked

greatly relieved to be able to push his revolver back in the holster and start across the square. He moved in a wide detour around the stalled wagon, as Adam Steele slowly lowered his arms to his sides.

This action caused the Winchester to jerk from its aim at Murchison to be trained on the Virginian. And some of the men who had begun to follow Dan's example in holstering their revolvers now wrenched them to the aim again: thumbed back the hammers to pose no more serious threat than before over a range of better than a hundred and twenty feet.

'I didn't say to——'

'So far, Sheriff, you haven't said one damn thing that makes any sense to him and me,' Steele cut in evenly on Fallows. And was aware of Clay Murchison nodding his agreement as he, too, brought his arms down to his sides. 'Except for having a woman come to tend to Zachery Petrie.'

The naming of the now quiet baby threatened to trigger another eruption of surprised talk among the men. But again the commanding tones of Len Fallows silenced all other voices.

'Mister, just why you've got Rosebud Petrie's child in that wagon is somethin' I ain't got the time to go into right now. Because right now I've got more important things on my mind. And I've wasted enough time with you and Clay Murchison.'

He stepped to the right and with head gestures signalled for the other members of the posse to move aside so that a clear way was opened up for Steele and Murchison to get to the law office doorway. The grave-digger, recovered from the exertion of the run and breathing easily, scuttled off the threshold: electing to come outside.

'Want you both to go into the cell,' the lawman went on. 'Want you both to know that if you don't do that— or give me any trouble while you're doin' it—then I'm goin' to shoot you down. It's that important to me. Move.'

Steele started away from the wagon, convinced Len Fallows was not voicing an idle threat. And his certainty about this was not based solely on the man's coldly determined tone of voice and the degree of resolve seen on his face. There was, too, the way in which his fellow citizens looked at him. All of them as apprehensive as the absent Dan had been. Seeing their sheriff in a frame of mind they had never experienced before.

'Hey, Steele, what——' Clay Murchison began to growl as he made haste to catch up with and walk alongside the Virginian.

'The man's in the same business as me, feller,' Steele broke in evenly. 'Maybe a late starter.'

'Len Fallows ain't never killed nobody in his life,' Murchison confirmed, and shared a glower of contempt between the lawman and the Virginian. Then did a double-take at Fallows from close quarters as he recognised what others had already identified. He swallowed hard then, down a throat constricted by fresh fear.

'You sayin' you're a killer, mister?' the youngest member of the posse asked incredulously, and turned his wide-eyed gaze from the impassive face of Steele to fix it on the grim-set features of Fallows to say: 'Ain't that what he said, Len?'

'He's for later, Harlan,' the lawman answered. 'You men go get mounted. Be with you in a minute.'

Steele stepped into the law office first. Murchison was close on his heels and Fallows was no more than a yard at the rear. He had passed the Winchester to another man and drawn the Frontier Colt from his holster now that he had his prisoners at close quarters.

There was just the single cell that took up one third of the space in the building: separated from the office area by a partition of floor-to-ceiling bars. It was not occupied and

93

the door at a midway point in the wall of bars was open. Again Steele was first through the doorway, to enter an area spartanly furnished with three wooden cots on which neatly folded blankets were stacked and a single tin bucket. The cell was as clean as the office and the whole interior of the building into which morning sunlight shafted smelled of a combination of wood polish and lye soap.

The Virginian went to the three by three feet window to gaze out on the town square as Fallows ordered Murchison to stand against the far wall, then clanged the barred door shut in the barred wall and turned the key in the lock.

'I've locked up a few prisoners in my time with the railroad!' Murchison said bitterly as Fallows moved to his desk and dropped the key in the drawer. 'Always told them why I was doin' it. Some of them turned out to be innocent.'

'On what I know now, until I get back to town, accessory to murder oughta cover it,' the lawman growled. And only now did his moustached face begin to lose the killing expression that had taken such a firm hold on the features perhaps a full minute ago.

'Murder?' Murchison exclaimed. 'Who was killed?'

'Your wife, you brutal bastard!' Fallows snarled, stepped out of the office and slammed the door violently behind him.

'Oh, dear God in heaven!' Murchison wailed, and slid down the wall until he was on his haunches: his gaunt face contorted by the anguish of grief and the agony of his diseased body protesting the unfamiliar attitude.

'You're all heart, feller,' Steele challenged evenly through the barred window as Fallows made to swing past, pushing the revolver into his holster.

The lawman paused and the grimace on his face expanded to a scowl as he growled in embittered tones: 'Chrissy

Murchison was all woman, mister! Until they hacked out of her most of what made her that way! Maybe when we get back, I'll let you see the body and you'll know why I'm so mad at anyone who had anythin' to do with killin' her!'

He started away from the window, taking long strides to get to where the men were starting to climb into their saddles. So he failed to hear Steele's soft spoken, taut-toned words that were barely audible in the cell against the sobbing of the distraught new widower.

'Reckon I've already got the picture, Sheriff. In black and white.'

9

By the time he reached the group it only remained for Len
Fallows to mount up; and he swung into the saddle of his
horse that had been unhitched from the livery stable rail,
and was held by the nervous old-timer who had returned
from bringing Arlene Forrester.

Then the posse started off at an immediate gallop—the
lawman taking the lead to head them off the north side
of the square through the gap between the law office and
the meeting hall. A group of men, mostly in the fifty to
sixty-five age group, with the single exception of the one
named Harlan who was not yet thirty. All of them garbed
for riding western trails and sitting saddles hung with the
essential accoutrements for a long trek over sparsely settled
country. Each had a repeater rifle in a boot as well as the
sixgun in a holster. Only the lawman and the youngest
member of the posse looked comfortable in their saddles
as the group set off to hunt down the trio of killers. And it
was not merely apprehension about what might lie ahead
of them that caused the rest of the men to be ill at ease.
Harlan was just as scared as they were: and Fallows was
burdened with a degree of fear, too. No, the other five
men were out of the habit of riding horseback. And they
seldom wore the clothes they had on now. Or packed a
gun. Steele guessed they were the merchants and business-
men of Providence. Pressed into doing a civic duty in the

aftermath of the kind of violent trouble that had never before been visited upon this usually peaceful town in the timber.

The pumping hooves exploded clouds of fine dust from the hard-packed surface of the square. And Arlene Forrester took pains to shield the face of Zachery Petrie from the motes that drifted toward the wagon as she crouched in the back tending to the baby. Because of the responsibility he felt toward the infant, Steele was relieved to see the woman was as black as Zachery. A short, heavily built Negress who looked to be in her forties or maybe was past fifty. She improvised a musical tone of voice the baby apparently found soothing, and spoke comforting nonsense to him as she changed the clothes he had soiled.

This sound of her voice did not reach to the window of the cell until the thudding of galloping hooves had faded into the distance north of town. And when it did, Murchison's grief had diminished to silent suffering. He did not even wince from physical pain as he eased awkwardly up off his haunches and sat on the centrally positioned cot. From where he peered at Steele as if he intended to pose a vitally important question. But his throat was closed even tighter now and he came near to choking before he surrendered to the temporary dumbness that Fallows' revelation had triggered.

'Save your breath, feller,' the Virginian told the anguished man who now rested his elbows on his knees and buried his face in his hands. 'My guess wouldn't be any better than yours.'

He returned his attention to the sun-bright square where the dust had now settled, and all that moved within his range of vision was the fleshy black woman as she continued to clean up Zachery Petrie in the back of the wagon. And the only sounds were of bird calls in the timber and the soft-spoken voice of Arlene Forrester. Until the slightly built, acne-faced man of thirty or so who had been digging a grave until he came on the run to this side of town wandered into view.

'Hey,' Steele called to him.

The man was startled, and when he snapped his head around and saw the face of the Virginian at the barred window he seemed about to bolt.

'I'll pay for a favour, feller,' Steele offered. And as he looked closely at the coveralled man for the first time he thought he could be mentally retarded.

'I ain't supposed to do nothin' but what Mr Marlow tells me, mister,' the slack-mouthed, bug-eyed, suddenly-sweating man replied.

'You won't get into trouble,' Steele assured the uneasy man, moderating his tone and trying for a warm smile. 'I don't want my wagon left out there in the middle of the square. So I'd like you to park it somewhere safe for me. The horses shouldn't have to stand out there in the open when the sun gets higher, either.'

'You get back to the grave-diggin' like the Reverend Marlow told you, Billy Baxter,' the black woman called. 'Don't you do nothin' that'll get you into hot water.'

'I'll pay a dollar, Billy,' Steele urged.

'And I'll do it for nothin',' Arlene Forrester countered as she climbed out of the back of the wagon and on to the seat. 'Get on and do what you been told, Billy Baxter.'

The retarded man had started to grin broadly when Steele had mentioned the dollar. Now he scowled and spoke a mild curse just loud enough to carry into the cell as the woman set the wagon rolling, tugging on the reins to head for the alley between the livery stable run by a man named Grout and the boarding house with a Rooms for Rent sign above the porch.

'Gotta go now, mister,' Billy Baxter said after a second or so of directing the malevolent scowl toward the broad back of the woman driving the wagon. Then he winked at Steele as he added: 'But maybe you'll need another kinda dollar favour later? After I'm through workin' for Mr Marlow?'

Then he set off at a loping run: across the square and into the trees at the south east corner. Obviously starting back along the short cut he had followed to get from the cemetery to the law office in time to warn the sheriff of the early morning visitors to town before the posse left Providence.

'That guy ain't got a full deck in his head, Steele,' Murchison said dully as he came to stand at the window. He spoke like a man with a sore throat. 'Got the mind of a kid no more than six, folks say. I'd guess there ain't nothin' much he wouldn't do for a buck. Long as he didn't forget what he was doin' while he was doin' it.'

'Yeah,' the Virginian responded absently after a glance at the haggard face of the man beside him: and guessing that Clay Murchison's self-control was fragile—that he was probably using talk as one way of holding himself together.

'Does all kindsa dirty jobs for anyone who'll pay him a few cents. Stronger than he looks. Does a good job so long as somebody watches over him. Lives in the stable out back of the parson's house.'

Zachery began to cry as the black woman emerged from the alley, leading the two horses taken from the wagon traces. As she took them into the livery stable, Murchison felt the need to sit down again. Did so on the nearest cot as he supplied:

'The nigger woman works at cleanin' chores all over town. Houses and stores and the bank. In here, too.'

He gestured with a hand to encompass the area beyond the wall of bars. Which was furnished with an uncluttered desk with a chair behind it and two in front, a chest of drawers, a hat stand hung with a duster coat and a potbellied stove set in a kerbed hearth. On the wall in back of the desk, across from the doorway and window, was a rifle rack that was unlocked and empty. And to one side of the stove chimney the wall opposite the cell area of the law office was hung with a map of Providence and the immediate surrounding area. The floor was boarded and the ceiling and walls were whitewashed. The scars of long and constant use could be seen in many places, but there was no more than a day's dust in the office and every wooden surface that could be polished had been: time and time again.

'Spoke highly of,' Murchison went on. 'But I bet she wasn't no better at the house keepin' than my Chrissy. Why, that girl used to run our place like . . .'

Steele ceased to pay more than a modicum of attention to Murchison as the man rambled on about the cleaning, cooking and needleworking skills of his wife. And although he continued to gaze out of the window, the sunlit scene beyond the bars served merely as a backdrop against which something might happen that would prove of use to him in getting out of this cell. Meantime he had to stare at some aspect of reality while he sought to keep a firm grip on his emotional stability. For he feared that if he dared to close his eyes, the rage that was so close to the surface would demand outlet.

And he might give vent to an animalistic bellow.

Or yank at the bars.

Overturn the cots and rip up the blankets.

Do injury to himself by smashing a gloved fist at the solid stone wall. Or to Clay Murchison by punching him instead of the wall. Or throttling him with his hands or the thuggee scarf. Maybe hack at him with the knife from the boot sheath. This wife-beating bigot who was now talking of his desperate need for a drink. But who remained in firm control of himself despite all that he was suffering. A pain wracked drunk without a drink. A husband whose last act toward a much-loved wife was to hit her. Who knew she had been brutally murdered. Who was in a prison cell, accused of contributing to her violent death. Without being told why.

And yet Adam Steele was within a hairsbreadth of losing control of his feelings. Because he was behind the same bars for some unspecified crime he knew he did not commit. This at a period of his life when he should have been through with the near lifelong business of killing. Should have been making the sunset ride. Looking for a piece of country much like that shown upon the map on the wall of this very building where he was imprisoned. A piece of country like that, anyway, with an important exception. There should be no people for many miles in every direction. No people like Rosebud Petrie and her baby. The Murchison couple. Parker and Tait and Ashton. A town sheriff and his bunch of uneasy deputies. A piece of country with just grass and trees and horses and a dog maybe. Steele's ranch house the only building for as far as it was possible to ride in a day. Flat out. Switching to a fresh horse every hour. For houses meant people, and people added up to trouble. Any way you looked at it.

While he gripped two of the window bars in tightly-clenched gloved hands, and felt the tautness of the skin as his face became hard set in a scowl of the kind of anger he could taste at the back of his throat, he was neither blind nor deaf to what took place around him. He had been aware of the Forrester woman leaving the livery and shuffling back into the alley. And knew when Zachery Petrie stopped crying. It was not lost on him when Clay Murchison abandoned talk and then took up private contemplation of his sense of guilt. After this for perhaps a full half minute the square remained deserted and the only sounds that disturbed the otherwise perfect silence of the town came from the birds in the trees that concealed every Providence building that was not on the square.

Then the black woman with the black baby in her fleshy

arms emerged from the alley and moved in a diagonal line toward the law office. She stopped opposite the barred window, four feet back from it. And at such close quarters Steele re-adjusted his estimate of her age. She was more than sixty, the lines inscribed by the passing years made less distinct by the way the excess flesh ballooned out the skin of her jet black, round and shiny face. There was not a trace of greyness in her sheened, tightly curled hair. She wore a shapeless work dress of grey denim, darned and patched and stained by many substances that would not wash out: for it had been recently laundered. And the woman herself smelled as fresh and clean as her clothing. The baby no longer smelled bad.

'I wanna thank you, mister,' she announced solemnly.

'For what, ma'am?' Steele asked. And felt a sense of gratitude to her. Just for being there with the baby. For unwittingly opening the safety valve that released the pressure of the futile rage that had built toward such a dangerous level.

She was suddenly startled and the Virginian thought that perhaps his face still betrayed an anger not directed at her. Until she explained:

'Mister, I just gets called Arlene 'round here. By the folks that don't mind so much about my colour. The likes of . . .' She gestured with her head to indicate the man who shared the cell with Steele. 'Other folks, they calls me lotsa different names.'

'Okay, Arlene.'

She smiled wanly as discomfort at the initial deference of a white man to her was eased. 'You bin takin' care of the baby for long, mister?'

'Yesterday afternoon.'

'He musta messed before. I guess you took care of that? And you musta fed him, too?'

Steele nodded and showed her a smile of his own. The kind that used to be boyish until the later years and their

102

harsher contents began to take such a heavy toll of his face. Said: 'Sometimes a man's gotta do what a woman usually does. But far as feeding him went, I could have been in real trouble. Just so far I could go as a wet nurse.'

She nodded, brightening the smile for a moment. Then was morosely silent for a moment more, before she asked: 'Rosebud? The baby's momma?'

'She's dead, Arlene.'

Tears welled into the dark eyes set in their starkly white surround. But they did not spill across the swollen cheeks. She sniffed wetly, and swallowed hard. 'Soon as they told me some man brung Zachery to town, I knew somethin' musta happened to Rosebud. How'd it happen, mister?'

'Were you and Rosebud Petrie——'

'She was my niece, mister,' Arlene Forrester broke in on him. 'Only daughter of my only brother who's a Gospel preacher back Kansas way. Brother Elroy, he was Christian enough to let Rosebud stay in his house until after the bastard baby got born. But pretty soon after that, he couldn't take no more. He threw them out, mister.' She gazed down into the face of the quiet infant, shaking her head slowly. 'They did some real hard travellin' to get here to me. And Rosebud was real sick when they got here to Providence?'

She returned her gaze to Steele's face, and in her eyes was an implied wish that it was the sickness that killed Rosebud Petrie.

'You just have to know that she's dead,' the Virginian replied. 'And buried as decently as the circumstances allowed. She lived long enough to ask me to take care of the baby.'

'And bring him here to me?'

'There wasn't that much time left to her, Arlene.'

The woman seemed ready to press for the details of the end of Rosebud Petrie, but then remorse overcame curiosity. And although she peered at the barred window, it was clear she did not see the head and shoulders of the man it framed as she reflected: 'I ought never to have let them leave my place. They did that soon as Rosebud figured she was over bein' sick. But I'd lost me some money-makin' chores while I took care of that girl. And that made her feel bad. She just upped and left while I was out workin'. Got back to the shack and this little baby and his momma was gone.'

'The hell with all that!' Murchison snarled as he joined Steele at the window again. And ignored the warning sidelong glance the Virginian directed toward him. 'Whatever you lost by nursin' your niece was chickenfeed, woman! Set against what I'll pay you if you'll open the door of this cell. And I figure Steele'll chip in some as well?'

'No, sir, Mr Murchison,' the woman hurried to reject the offer. 'I couldn't do that. I likes livin' here in this town. I gets by fine cleanin' up after folks who ain't got nothin' against me for no reason. I put the horses in Harlan Grout's livery and you folks'll have to see him about payin' for the stablin' later. And I got the wagon off the town square like I was asked to.'

There was fear in her fast-talking voice and now she began to back step away from the cell window and direct furtive glances to left and right: like she felt she would be in trouble if anyone saw her outside the law office.

'Hey, come back here, you crazy——'

'Shut up, feller,' Steele cut in on his cellmate. And immediately softened his tone as he switched his attention back to the woman outside. 'Okay, Arlene. I don't want to cause you any trouble. But come back here and tell me . . .'

She had continued to back off from the window. Then began to shake her head with increasing rapidity: refusing to agree to anything that might be asked of her. The tears she had held back on now started to course across her cheeks. And she whirled and hurried across the square as the clop of hooves and the rattle of wheels sounded on the street that started into the trees directly opposite the law office. She made it just as some horsemen, two buggies and a group of women on foot appeared on the street.

Murchison spat at the clean floor of the cell and complained sourly: 'Shit, Steele, you sure wasted time with that black cow.'

Once again the Virginian had to make a conscious effort to control the urge to violent temper as the older man lowered himself back on the nearest cot. Needed to force himself to keep looking out through the bars instead of whirling to face the older man. His voice rang with a strained tone in his own ears when he responded: 'You were sure a hell of a lot faster in getting her to turn tail and run, feller.'

Murchison, whose grief had diminished to an extent that left him painfully aware of his aching joints and his need for a drink, did not say anything for several stretched seconds. And in this time Steele directed just a single fleeting glance at him: saw the kind of suffering he endured and returned his cold-eyed gaze to the scene through the bars. The square was more crowded now, as the citizens of Providence and people from the out-of-town farms came off the street to the south. There were children too, dawdling at first but then scurrying toward the schoolhouse when a handbell began to ring. This as their elders headed for the stores and business premises: owners, employees or customers.

Only the younger children chattered happily and laughed as they made their way across the square in the bright, warm sunlight: impervious to everything that did not occupy their thoughts at the moment. Everyone else was pre-occupied with what they had heard of the unfamiliar trouble that had come to Providence earlier this fine new

105

day. And it took Adam Steele just a few moments to realise where the violence had erupted. For the First Providence Town Bank remained firmly closed up after all the other business premises were opened. And few people failed to spare the shuttered building an uneasy glance.

Similarly, few did not look toward the law office with expressions that suggested various feelings of ill-will for its current occupants.

'You're right,' Clay Murchison allowed morosely. 'Your way was better with her. But I could've told you there wasn't no chance she'd do anythin' to set Providence folks against her.' He sighed deeply. 'Just wish you'd gotten her to talk about what happened to Chrissy. And why me and you are gettin' some of the blame for it.'

'Whatever happened, it happened at the bank, looks like,' Steele said.

He turned from the window and went to sit on the centre cot. Swung his feet up off the floor and lay back, using the heap of blankets for a pillow. He saw Murchison get gingerly to his feet and go to the window before he tipped his hat forward over his face to block out most of the sunlight. Then, for many moments it was serenely peaceful in the law office as the sounds of the town entered unobtrusively now that the clanging of the hand-bell had stopped.

Until the man at the window growled sourly: 'Shit, I can almost smell Harry Krim's fine corn liquor from here.' He spat through the bars on to the dirt outside. Then, just as Steele was about to give in to a comfortable weariness that had come in the wake of tension, he was wrenched back to the reality of his circumstances when Murchison bellowed: 'Hey, you people out there! What the hell's happenin' around here? Why's Fallows and his cronies locked me up? What happened to Chrissy? I didn't do nothin' to her! I sure didn't do nothin' that killed her!'

'Sure you did, you brutal——' a woman began to respond, shrill with righteous anger.

'Leave it be, Blanche!' a man cut in on her, his tone grim.

'Yeah, let the drunken sot stew for awhile!' another woman urged.

'Damn right! Sit in there without no liquor and think about how you treated that fine wife you had, you blackhearted sonofabitch!'

The handbell began to clang again, urgently striving to drown out the malevolent tones of this husky-voiced man. Then the strident noise ended abruptly and another woman censured:

'Please! There are children within earshot, Mr Withers! How am I expected to teach them good manners and what is decent when you and others——'

There was some subdued talk that evidently placated the dismayed schoolteacher, and then the sounds that drifted into the law office were muted again as the townspeople went about their daily business with the same brand of undemonstrative uneasiness as before Murchison's outburst. But then the man at the window shattered the peace of Providence once again.

'Just one more thing, you people!' he yelled and there was grim resolve in his voice now. 'I ain't gonna have my wife buried in this lousy town! So somebody better go tell Holy Joe Marlow and that idiot Baxter they're wastin' their time and sweat with the grave diggin'! You hear me?'

That no-one responded with either word or sign was evident from the way in which Murchison whirled away from the window and slammed down on the side of the nearest cot. The violence of the move caused him pain, and he groaned. Then he directed a baleful look at Steele who had raised the hat off his face to watch the other man's reaction.

'She was my wife,' Murchison defended, wearied by his

107

anguish and pain. 'I figure I got the right to say where she's laid to rest.'

'Sure you have,' Steele agreed.

'I know I didn't treat her like I should've a lot of the time, but——'

'Think about it, feller,' Steele interjected on what sounded like it could be the preamble to a maudlin monologue.

'You figure I ain't been thinkin' about it, mister?' Murchison snarled.

'I meant instead of shooting off your mouth. Which won't help because no-one can shout loud enough to wake the dead.'

'Could I use a drink,' the older man muttered, licking his lips and then drawing the back of a hand across the wetness left by his tongue.

Steele lowered the Stetson back on his face and drawled: 'You don't have a hope, I reckon. So best to keep thinking about your wife and what's to happen to the body.'

'Goin' to bury Chrissy on the place.'

'Fine. That's settled, feller. Same as it is for us.'

'Uh?'

'We've got no place else but here to rest in peace.'

10

The Virginian was sure he would have been able to drift easily into sleep if he had been alone in the cell of the Providence law office. Even though it was still quite early in the morning, after a night when he had been deeply asleep for a lot of the time. Because he had slept most soundly in unnatural unconsciousness, and that brand of induced rest did not do a man any good at all. His head still thudded dully from the blow with the gun and the kick. And maybe the ache was sharpened by the bad memories that plagued his mind? Sharpened, too, by the frustrations of being unable to do anything yet about settling the scores that these memories insisted he owed. But it would have been possible to close his mind to the traumatic recent past and resist the temptation to contemplate the violent future that he intended should follow his release. And, this achieved, the pain in his head would have diminished against the somnolent sounds that filtered through the bars into the clean, warm, relatively comfortable cell.

But he was not alone. And his fellow prisoner was in no frame of mind to resign himself quietly to a situation he was as yet helpless to change. For Clay Murchison paced the cell, moving back and forth along the length of the barred wall. And occasionally the regular setting down of his booted feet on the cement floor was counterpointed by a grim-toned curse directed at a target only he knew. Then sometimes he would mutter discernible snatches of talk that revealed his discontent was variously caused by the townspeople in general, the sheriff in particular, the murder of his wife or the lack of liquor.

The man had reason enough to feel so troubled, Steele acknowledged. Reduced as he had been from a railroad lawman, proud of the fine job he did for so long, to what he was now. An embittered man made old before his time by physical pain and maybe the harder to endure suffering of being impotent and married to a beautiful young wife. A wife he had mistreated to the point where she felt forced to run off in the dead of night to beg help from a passing stranger. Ran off while he lay slumped in a drunken stupor. And now she was dead. Killed by three other strangers. How this came to be he did not know. Nor why he was locked up in this cell, accused of a share of the blame for her violent end.

Yeah, the Virginian thought. Clay Murchison had been handed the dirty ends of a few sticks. So what the hell did it matter if he had taken a grip on some of them without even putting up a fight? He, Steele, had been guilty of doing that every now and then. Probably most people were the same. It was just that some were better able to handle their problems than others. Like he, Adam Steele . . ? Like hell! Back at the bank of the stream in the valley just a few short hours ago he had not merely yelled at the top of his voice nor tried pacing up and down to relieve the pressure of emotional turmoil. He had drawn the knife and come close to committing an act of bloody violence. And there had been countless times in the past when he had not held back with a knife or a gun or whatever weapon was to hand.

Just as he would not stop short of the ultimate act of revenge against the three men who had forced him to grasp the dirty end of this particular stick. Just as soon as he was out from behind these bars and free to go after the buck-toothed Stan Tait, Denny Parker with the crooked nose and the scar-faced Lonnie Ashton.

If they were still alive and free after the posse returned to town . . .

Which thought brought him full circle to where he had started to be irritated by Clay Murchison's restlessness: the premise that it was pointless to expend nervous energy on a set of circumstances you were powerless to change. A man might just as well rest up. So that if the situation altered and he regained control of it, he would be fresh and ready to react to whatever new problems came his way.

He raised his back up off the cot then. Pushed the hat on to the top of his head and swung his feet to the floor. When he began the move it had been in his mind to tell Murchison to quit the pacing and take it easy for awhile. But even before he looked up at the man, he abandoned this notion. Different people had different ways of handling what ailed them. And it really did not irk Steele too much that the older man needed to keep on the move and occasionally give vocal vent to his feelings.

Then, when Murchison turned at the window end of his limited walking space, Steele saw that the man might soon be forced to take a rest. For he looked totally drained—physically and mentally exhausted. With eyes that seemed more deeply sunk into his skull, cheeks that appeared hollower than before and a skin pallor that was almost death-like. Also, beads of sweat stood out on his brow and runnels of salt moisture trickled across his scrawny neck. And he was trembling as if the flesh out of which the sweat squeezed felt ice-cold to him.

He curtailed the pacing and leaned his back against the wall beside the window when he saw Steele looking at him. And showed a mirthless grin that exposed the full lengths of his teeth but failed to put even a spark of life in the dead-looking eyes. Said in a tone of voice that sounded as weak as he looked: 'I can see me in you, Steele. The way I used to be. You'll see this through to the end, I bet. We made a deal, didn't we? Hell, I feel sicker than I ever did before. I feel sick enough to cash in, Steele. If that happens . . . If I get too sick to carry on . . . Even if I don't cash in . . . You'll get them three that . . .'

He swayed to one side, then the other as his mouth hung slackly open with saliva drooling out. His eyelids blinked rapidly.

'If the posse doesn't—' Steele started as he realised a considerable amount of time had gone by while he was sprawled out on the cot. That he was not squinting simply because of the contrast between the shade under his hat and the brilliance of the sunlight that shafted into the law office through the barred and the glazed window. The sun was a lot higher and brighter than it had been when he withdrew into his private world of introspection.

Murchison made a sound of disgust and pursed his lips. Gathered the drool into a spit that he ejected force- fully. This as he swung toward the wall of bars, so that the stream of saliva hit the boarded area of the floor in the law office. Then he had to clench his fists around two of the bars to remain upright as he snarled: 'Bunch of friggin' amateurs, Steele! That's what them men are! They couldn't track a train down a railroad! And if they get lucky and find them killers . . . Well, I figure they'll wind up unlucky. Ain't one of them can shoot worth a damn. Shit, there's only young Harlan Grout can see much beyond the end of his nose without needin' eyeglasses!'

Steele said nothing as he rose and went to look at the scene beyond the barred window. Aware that Murchison was watching him with eyes that were more alive now. This as the older man—still mad—spoke with a greater degree of clarity. So that it seemed the silence Steele had forced upon the man had been bad for him. Clay Murchison just was not able to face up to what troubled him while he was isolated: even from a man who felt so little sympathy for him. But could Steele feel a greater degree of compassion for him since he had gone as far as he was able to comply with the Virginian's hard-toned advice? Done this to the extent where he had come close to sinking into a state of dementia before he felt compelled to say what was in his troubled mind again. And the talk acted to relieve the build-up of tension.

'Easy, feller,' Steele drawled, and spared a glance for Murchison, who was staring at him. And hardened his tone to say with a degree of conviction he did not entirely feel: 'I reckon it could be it's just a drink you're dying for?'

'You're well named, Steele!' the older man snarled, and the Virginian felt a sense of relief that he had called it right. 'Hard as steel is what you are. Ain't even an ounce of pity in you, is my guess.'

'Reckon you've got me weighed up real well,' Steele said as he returned his attention to the square outside the window, which was baking under a sun that was close to the noon peak of its arc across the cloudless sky.

There was now very little activity in this downtown area of Providence. For the morning shopping was done, school was not yet out for the midday recess, and men like Harlan Grout who ran the livery were riding with the posse. It seemed like the bank had not opened at all this morning, and Steele wondered if the banker was one of those who had been deputised for posse duty by Fallows.

'You're right, damn you!' Murchison growled abruptly as a sudden burst of happy shouting out of Steele's range of vision signalled morning school was over.

'About what?' the Virginian asked, as he saw a throng of children spill on to the square and advance across it, most running or playing fast-moving games, and a few ambling along like they had plenty of time to get home for the midday meal.

'Not to soft soap me. That's where Chrissy went wrong, sometimes. Sometimes when I got to feelin' real sorry for myself, she'd say how she understood and she'd try to treat me like . . . Hell, like I was one of them little kids I hear out there I guess. That used to rile me. A man like I am is best left alone when he gets to wallowin' in not bein' the kinda man he used to be. Because he can't raise it for his wife, or he hurts in every joint of his lousy body, because he has to have a drink to make him forget about . . . Shit, you know what I mean, Steele. If someone had tried to soft-talk me when I was like I used to be . . .'

'Sure,' Steele allowed as his attention was caught by the opening of a door in the shade of the boarding house porch across at the south east corner of the square. Then he recognised the slightly-built figure of Billy Baxter standing on the threshold: the mentally retarded man apparently waiting there nervously until the last of the children had gone from the square before he ventured across the porch and down the two steps. He carried a cloth-draped tray which he brought toward the law office, his tongue sticking out the side of his mouth as a sign of the concentration needed as he struggled to keep the tray level. 'This time it's you who's right. I know what you mean. I'd be the same.'

There was a quality of detachment in the way Steele responded and Murchison came to the window, intrigued by what was holding the Virginian's attention outside. Growled in a disappointed tone:

'Be grub, mister. Blanche Knight who runs the roomin' house gets paid outta the county purse to feed the prisoners.' He backed off to sit on the nearest cot again, and added after a grimace of pain: 'She don't get rich on it. On account of there ain't hardly ever any prisoners in here to be fed.'

Outside, a woman greeted cheerfully: 'Good afternoon, Billy. I hope things are going well for you?'

The coveralled man halted abruptly and his acne-scarred face showed a frown of apprehension as the tray tilted dangerously. Then his expression did not alter much after he had stabilised his burden, and he remained rooted to the spot while he looked toward the woman striding across the square in his direction. A tall, thin, grey-haired woman of something over fifty with a sharp-featured face. She was neatly garbed in a black dress made of a fabric that looked to be too heavy for the hot weather; but she seemed cool enough. Her carriage was erect and quick and she polished her eyeglasses with a very white handkerchief as she advanced on the nervous Baxter. Steele thought her appearance was as schoolma'amish as her voice had been when he first heard it earlier in the day.

'Pretty good, Miss Attwood,' the man with the tray blurted. Then he gasped and jerked the tray to the side, almost tipping to the ground what was concealed beneath the cloth. This as the schoolteacher replaced the spectacles on her face, halted and reached out to lift a corner of the cloth. 'It's grub for the prisoners in the lock-up, Miss Attwood!'

'I realise that, Billy,' the mildly perturbed woman answered. 'I simply wished to see in advance what it is Mrs Knight has fixed for lunch today. But I can wait.'

She recommenced her near regal progress from one corner of the square to the opposite one, and revealed no sign that she heard when Baxter called after her:

'It's fried chicken and baked sweet potato, Miss Attwood. Smells and looks real good!'

'And sounds good, too,' Steele murmured as Baxter stuck out his tongue again and continued his tentative progress toward the law office.

'And it'll taste that way,' Murchison said without relish. 'Chrissy and me, we stayed at Blanche Knight's place

115

while we waited for some of the house-buildin' materials to arrive. She's a fine cook, that woman.'

Billy Baxter had some trouble getting into the law office. Until he worked it out that it was best to set the tray down on the ground before swinging open the door. Then he carefully put it down on the floor inside the office and closed the door. Only when he had come to within six feet of the barred door in the wall of bars did he look at the prisoners. Then came to a standstill and assured them:

'Grub don't cost you nothin'. And Mrs Knight, she give me a nickel to bring it over to here. So ain't no charge to you for that.'

'Sure,' Murchison growled.

'You want to put it down on the floor again and slide it under,' Steele suggested, gesturing toward the base of the door where there was a gap some twelve inches deep for just such a purpose.

'Depends,' Baxter countered, and a look of cunning spread across his lean, sun-burnished, red-pitted and yellow-pimpled face.

'Uh?' Murchison asked with a sneer.

'Depends on what, feller?' Steele augmented.

Baxter giggled. Then earnest as he replied: 'Depends on if you wanna pay for somethin' extra to the grub.'

'I'll pay for a bottle of Harry Krim's rye whiskey,' Murchison promised with scant hope.

Baxter grimaced and chided: 'Shoot, Mr Murchison, you know Mr Krim won't sell me nothin' stronger than sarsap——'

'What else have you got under the cloth, feller?' Steele asked.

'You'll pay?'

Steele took from a hip pocket a once-folded sheaf of bills. A five and three ones. Just carrying money that he would not have been too put out to have stolen from him if Parker and his partners had found it. By far the greater

116

portion of what he was worth, in cash money and gold nuggets, was aboard the hay wagon with his other possessions: and he had checked to see that the trio of intruders on his night camp had not stolen this. Did so before Murchison and he broke camp to head for Providence.

Now he fanned out the four bills and held them like a poker hand after a discard to draw one. And gazed fixedly over them into the suddenly eager face of Baxter as he answered: 'Not a cent to look. Have to see what you have there. So I can judge its worth.'

Clay Murchison forgot his need of a drink, and confined his response to rheumatic pain to a silent grimace as he rose from the cot and came to stand alongside Steele at the barred door: suddenly intrigued by the proposition he had not taken seriously before.

'How much is there, mister?' Baxter asked, and the tongue that he stuck out now moved back and forth along his top and then bottom lip.

'Eight bucks, feller.'

'Wow! I ain't never been paid anythin' like that much before!'

He broke off and was suddenly anxious. Like he was having doubts about the wisdom of what he planned. But then he abruptly dropped to his haunches and set the tray down on the floor. And with a histrionic flourish he drew the cloth off the tray. Grinned through the aromatic steam that rose from the two well laden plates. Enjoying the reactions of the men in the cell.

As Murchison demanded huskily: 'How'd you get one of my revolvers, Billy?'

And Steele asked evenly: 'Is it still loaded, feller?'

The man of thirty or so with the mind of a young child nodded vigorously, suddenly excited. 'Picked up your belt and holsters with the guns in them from where you tossed them down like Mr Fallows told you, Mr Murchison,' he replied, talking quickly. 'Everyone else forgot it, looked

117

like. So when the black woman took the wagon down into the alley over by the livery stable, I just grabbed your belt and stuff and put it under my work clothes. Loaded if it was when I got it. I don't know how to take the shells outta a gun. I got the other one and the belt in my room at Mr Marlow's house. I didn't guess you'd need more than the one to get outta the lock-up.'

'It's worth the whole eight dollars,' Steele told the fast-talking man.

'You can keep the other gun, Billy,' Murchison hurried to add. 'And the belt too, if you want.'

'Gee, thanks!' Baxter acknowledged, grinning broadly as he came erect and began to push the tray toward the gap beneath the door with his scuffed boot. Promised: 'And I won't use it anyplace near town. Wouldn't want to hurt nobody. Wouldn't want nobody to know I helped you to get outta the lock-up, neither.' He giggled. 'Or maybe I could finish up in there, uh?'

The tray inched its leading side under the door, and Steele pushed his arm through the bars, extending the money in his gloved hand toward the by-turns giggling and grinning Billy Baxter. This as Murchison, his own excitement transcending pain, went down into a crouch so he could reach under the door: his splayed hand going for the Remington that lay between the two plates on the tray.

'I got it, Steele.'

Baxter's expression was suddenly anxious and he thrust out a hand, grabbed the money and wrenched the bills out of the loosened grip of Steele.Then his anxiety swelled to fear as he gasped: 'No! It ain't supposed to be this way! You ain't supposed to use the gun until Mr Fallows and the rest of them get back from——'

He took two backward steps and became rooted to the spot. Out of the reach of the men behind the bars, but within easy range of the sixgun that Murchison aimed at him, the hammer thumbed back and his finger curled to the trigger. The enormity of Baxter's awesome fear forced him to curtail what he was saying and left his mouth flapping open and closed soundlessly while his wide eyes filled with a tacit plea for the men behind the bars to follow his plan.

'Easy, Billy,' Steele urged softly, and sent a sidelong glance at the heavily-breathing Murchison as he added: 'You, too, feller.

'*Now* I feel almost fine, Steele,' the older man growled, his eyes fixed upon the pathetically horrified face of Baxter with the same rock steadiness as the gun muzzle threatened the skinny belly. 'Yeah, Billy, you do like the man tells you and take it easy, uh?'

'Look, I don't want no money!' Baxter implored, and hurled the bills away from him. They hit the bars and fluttered to the floor on his side.

This as Steele returned his gaze to the almost weeping man: after he had glanced outside to see if the raising of voices had attracted attention to the law office. Within his range of vision all was deserted and as quiet as before. He reminded the agitated man: 'You've come this far. Now we need you to do us one more favour. And I'll pay you extra when I get out of here.'

'Please . . .?' Now tears did begin to course down the pitted and blotched cheeks of the child in an adult's frame.

'Just need you to go to the sheriff's desk, Billy,' the Virginian went on in an even but insistent tone. 'Open the top drawer on the right and bring the ring of keys you find inside.'

'No!'

Baxter looked on the point of whirling and racing for the door. But when Murchison pushed the gun out through two bars, reducing the range by some three feet, the terrified man found he was unable to get his feet free of the floor.

'It's all right, Billy,' Steele assured. 'After you've brought us the keys, you can leave. We won't let ourselves out until you've had time to get clear. Won't anyone know you had a hand in setting us free, far as we're concerned.'

'I can't.' Baxter had broken out into a sweat and was clenching and unclenching his shaking hands. 'I can't do it, mister.'

'Sure you can, Billy.'

'You damn well better, you halfbrained, crazy sonofa——'

'Shut your mouth!' Steele snarled with a glowering glance at Murchison.

'I'll kill him for sure! I'll kill you, Billy! My Chrissy's dead and the bastards that done for her are ridin' free. I don't give a shit what I have to do to get outta this place and go after them killers!'

'Please!' Baxter cried, and ran a sleeved arm across his tear- and sweat-wet face. 'It wasn't supposed to be——'

'Sure, Billy,' Steele cut in, and despite the childish tones and attitudes of Baxter he found it difficult to adjust amid a turmoil of conflicting emotions to the knowledge that he was in effect addressing a child of six or seven. 'Look, I've told you what to do. And how you'll be safe after you've done it. Nobody in town will know it was you who brought us the gun and——'

'Either that or you'll be dead!' Murchison snarled. 'Count of ten, you hear? If you can count in that lame-brain you got, that is?'

Steele knew he could take the gun away from Clay Murchison with ease. The man was old and pained: and for the moment had tunnel vision only for the terrified boy-man who stood trembling in front of the revolver. But it was not only the risk that the gun might go off and explode a bullet into Baxter by accident that held the Virginian back from making a move. He knew that his promise of safety was not enough to motivate Billy Baxter

120

into doing what he asked. The frightened man needed the threat of the aimed Remington to force him into action.

'One,' Murchison said. And moved the gun for a moment. Made a quick gesture with it toward the desk. 'Two, Billy. I ain't foolin'. Three. Not with my Chrissy dead. Four.'

'Okay! Okay, I'll do it! Please don't shoot me!'

He started to back away as he spoke. Then turned, but kept his head twisted so that his horrified gaze remained fixed upon the gun. He banged into the desk and vented a startled gasp. Then looked at what he was doing when Steele reminded him:

'Top drawer to the right, Billy.'

Baxter needed to raise both his shaking hands and study them for a moment to jog his under-developed memory. Was correct at the first try.

'Atta boy,' Murchison murmured on an expulsion of pent-up breath. And he withdrew his gun hand back through the bars, as a sound akin to a laugh forced a way out of his throat.

'The keys, Billy,' Steele urged as the man at the desk peered into the open drawer and screwed his head around one way and then the other: to study what he saw from different angles.

Baxter seemed not to hear what the Virginian said. Appeared to have abruptly withdrawn into a private world that left him totally unaware of the present reality while for stretched seconds he was insulated from fear.

'Five!' Murchison snarled. 'Five, damn you! Quit stallin' and——'

'Oh my!' Baxter groaned, and was suddenly gripped by a greater fear than before. Its cause unconnected with Steele and Murchison and the gun and the potential repercussions if the people of Providence found out what he had done. This obvious as he reached into the drawer with both hands and took out a sheaf of papers. The ring

121

of keys slid off what looked like a dozen or so wanted flyers and rattled on the wooden base of the drawer. Baxter hurriedly glanced through the papers, shaking his head and venting low groans.

'I said to quit sta——' Murchison started.

'I gotta go!' the mentally deficient man cut in without looking toward the barred wall. 'Oh my!'

Suddenly he hurled the papers to the floor, came out from behind the desk and lunged across the law office toward the door. Utterly unconcerned about the danger of being shot down because he was no longer aware of it. His child's mind was elsewhere and nothing mattered to him except the terrifying images that filled his mind.

'Shit, you crazy——' Murchison roared and started to thrust the gun between the bars again as Baxter reached the door and wrenched it open.

Steele half turned and punched a fist into the crook of Murchison's outstretched arm. Forced the arm to bend and swing the revolver away from the fleeing target as a shot exploded from its muzzle. The bullet smashed into the wall at the side of the open doorway and ricocheted behind the man who powered out over the threshold. This as Murchison vented a shrill scream of pain as his forearm was almost snapped by the momentary pressures of the bars.

'What the——' the grimacing man began to demand. And dragged his punished arm back inside the cell, to clutch at it with his other hand.

'The lock, feller,' Steele snarled at him through gritted teeth. 'And it better not take more than five shells to free it!'

Murchison's agonised expression had begun to change into a threatening scowl as he transferred the Remington to the hand of his uninjured arm. But the logic of what the Virginian said suddenly penetrated through his mounting rage and neutralised it.

'Shit, that's right!' he rasped.

The tautly-spoken words sounded against a barrage of shouted questions from out on the square. But neither man took the time to glance out of the barred window.

'Hold it,' Steele warned as Murchison pushed the revolver muzzle toward the tongue of the lock between the door and the bar that formed the frame.

He whirled, gathered up the folded blankets from two cots and stood alongside the other man to wrap them around the gun and the hand that held it. Nodded as he raised a foot and pushed it against the horizontal bar at the base of the door.

The voices sounded much louder out on the square. And Murchison fired the Remington. Just two shots, their reports muffled by the blankets. Then the door swung open under the pressure of Steele's foot. The would-be ricochets dropped harmlessly to the floor as the Virginian tossed aside the blankets that reeked of gunsmoke.

Murchison sent the tray and its plates of food skittering across the floor amid the discarded bills as he lunged out of the cell. He did not pause on the threshold of the law office and his sudden appearance on the square totally silenced the voices that had started to falter in the wake of the two muffled gunshots.

'Get back!' he bellowed. 'I'll kill anyone that tries to stop me!'

His running feet thudded on the ground in a cadence which, like the strength in his voice, signalled that his elation at being free acted to numb the pain of exertion.

Steele heard this and registered it in his pre-occupied mind, along with the mixture of sounds as the townspeople reacted to Clay Murchison's threat. But he did not even glance through the window or open doorway as he moved among the debris on the floor of the no-longer neat law office: searching for what it was that had triggered Billy Baxter's panic.

He had no logical reason to think that whatever had

sent the mentally retarded man running scared should mean anything to him. It was just a hunch.

He soon saw that an earlier hunch had been correct: the papers Baxter had scattered across the floor were wanted posters. Some simply carried printed names and descriptions of men who had committed a variety of crimes in various towns or counties or states or territories. Others were illustrated with sketches of the wanted men's faces.

Steele had to stoop and turn over some of the flyers that had floated to the floor face down. And it was one of these that drew a grunt of mild satisfaction from him. For it showed remarkably good likenesses of Parker, Tait and Ashton. And proclaimed them as convicted murderers who had escaped from the prison where they were scheduled to be hanged. The poster was issued by the Territorial Government of New Mexico.

'Oh!' a woman exclaimed softly as she came to a standstill on the threshold of the law office.

Steele looked across at her as he set the wanted flyer down on the desk. Touched the brim of his hat with a gloved forefinger and greeted evenly: 'Good afternoon to you . . . Miss Attwood, isn't it?'

The schoolteacher's surprise became apprehension, and she had to swallow hard before she was able to force out: 'Oh, I thought that perhaps . . ? After the shots . . ? And only Mr Murchison came out . . ? It seemed there was a chance you were injured? Since it was so quiet in here?'

Steele emerged from behind the desk and went briefly down on his haunches to retrieve the money Baxter had rejected. The grey-haired, sharp-featured woman in the black dress watched him nervously. Then backed out on to the square as he came upright, pocketed the bills and advanced on the doorway.

'Nobody was hurt,' he told her. 'I had a little reading to catch up on.'

She was perplexed by the cryptic comment. Then spread

across her face a disapproving frown, such as she might direct at one of her students who had misbehaved. And censured the Virginian: 'You men should not have taken advantage of poor Billy Baxter. He may look like a full grown adult but he's actually a child of——'

'I know, Miss Attwood,' Steele broke in on her as he came to a halt on the threshold of the law office. And took a deep breath of the hot air of early afternoon: relished the fragrances from the surrounding timber in the wake of the pungent odour of gunsmoke mixed with fried chicken that filled the office. He needed to crack his eyes against the brilliant glare of the sun as he raked his gaze over the square. As he did so, asked: 'Be grateful if you'll tell me where the Reverend Marlow lives?'

The woman's upright bearing became suddenly rigid with a combination of shock and determination as she started to respond: 'I have absolutely no intention of giving any form of aid to a man who has broken out of——'

She interrupted herself with a gasp, and fear froze her as she was instantly gripped by a much deeper degree of shock. This as Adam Steele dropped into a half stoop and his right hand delved into the split on that side of his pants leg. Then he powered up, the knife from the boot sheath clutched in his gloved hand. Took two strides to reach the woman, his hand held high to push the sun-glinting blade to within an inch of her throat.

The entire series of moves had taken no longer than three seconds. And perhaps two more seconds went by in the hot, tense silence as Miss Attwood leaned backwards from her narrow waist, her face contorted by horror and her wrinkled flesh pulsing under the threat of the knife. Then, his voice rasping out through tightly clenched teeth, Steele said:

'Schoolteacher, I need a little religious instruction. And you'd best tell me where the local preacher lives. Or else it could be this morning you'll have endeth your last lesson.'

11

The Providence schoolma'am shuddered and found her voice. Accused the Virginian: 'This is stupid. And you are not a stupid man, I think.'

Steele felt the white-hot rage that had triggered the violence suddenly contract to a ball of ice that lodged at the pit of his stomach. His tone of voice was a lot less harsh when he replied: 'I reckon you're right on both counts, Miss Attwood. A word to the wise, though. Tell me what I want to know.'

She sighed. 'The other side of town. House right next door to the church. There's a sign in the church porch that explains this.'

Her tone was faintly supercilious but she remained in the grip of tension until he withdrew the blade from against her throat, nodded in acknowledgement of what she had told him and half crouched to slide the knife back in the boot sheath. Then side-stepped and raised both hands to cup them at his mouth as an improvised bullhorn. Yelled:

'Reckon you all saw what happened! Your schoolteacher is a little ruffled, that's all! I could have hurt her, but I didn't!'

'Are you all right, Lavinia?' a woman called from just inside the threshold of the boarding house.

Elsewhere around the square, there were people on the

roof-shaded sidewalk out front of the line of stores. A man stood in the doorway of the stage line depot and a woman peered through a window in the façade of the same building. Some of these watchers had been out in the open in the full glare of the sun when the Virginian first showed himself at the law office entrance. But then had scuttled back. Probably they had reacted in much the same way when Murchison emerged from the doorway brandishing the Remington. Now the man was nowhere in sight.

'Yes, Blanche, I'm very well!' the tall, slender woman in black responded, as she turned with just a trace of unsteadiness to survey the same scene as Steele.

A sudden sound caused the couple out front of the law office to look sharply to the left. Beyond the façade of the building that housed the Providence Post-Despatch toward The Golden State Saloon. Where, for just a second or so, all that moved was the tail of a sorry looking grey gelding that was hitched to the rail there. The saddled animal standing in the full heat of the blistering sun. But then the batwings were pushed open and the tall figure of Clay Murchison came out. Still toting the Remington. His jacket was unbuttoned, so that the side pockets were better able to accommodate pint bottles of liquor.

He was no longer elated. And it seemed likely he had taken a long drink from another bottle as a different kind of fuel to power actions that took no account of pain. But he was not yet drunk: remained sharply alert to potential danger as he crossed from the saloon doorway to the disconsolate gelding, unhitched the reins from the rail and swung up astride the saddle. Constantly scanned the surrounding buildings and timber with a brand of intelligent diligence far removed from paranoic fear.

And as Steele watched the man who had become old before his time achieve this, he guessed that Clay Murchison was feeling something like he did in the good old days of being a railroad company lawman.

'Agreed to pay Roland Decker a fair price to rent his mount!' the grim-faced man in the saddle yelled as he backed the horse away from the rail and turned him. 'I'm no more a horsethief than a killer!'

'Just get the hell away from here, Murchison!' a man snarled from within the saloon.

Murchison ignored the challenge and his gaze lingered for no longer on the batwing doors than on any other area of the square as he offered the Virginian: 'I'll cover you far as the alley where the nigger woman took your wagon, Steele. Then you're on your own. Same as I'll be. Like I should've been all along.' He spat. 'After Chrissy took off.'

'I'm grateful, feller,' Steele said evenly. 'But I reckon I'll make out on my own from right now.'

Murchison sent another globule of saliva at the sun-baked ground and raked his gaze over the square in a manner that patently implied the spit was a sign of his feelings for the town of Providence and everyone in it. Then he thudded his spurred heels into the flanks of the doleful gelding and yelled at the animal to command an instant gallop. Swung in a wide arc away from The Golden State Saloon, across in front of the newspaper building and law office and then off the square by way of the street that ran north.

Both Steele and Lavinia Attwood needed to crack their eyes almost closed and compress their lips against the assault of fine dust kicked up by the pumping hooves.

'Good riddance to bad rubbish!' Blanche Knight taunted against the diminishing thud of galloping hooves.

'Len Fallows ain't gonna like it that no-one tried to stop him!' a man predicted in sour tones from inside the saloon. Not the same one who had urged Murchison to leave town.

'He was crazy angry, Harry,' this one countered as the two of them came out of the batwinged doorway. 'I figure

128

he really meant what he said about blastin' anyone that got in his way.'

'There is no doubt of that, I am quite certain, Mr Decker,' the schoolteacher contributed.

This as the man and woman from the stage depot came outside, and a half dozen people stepped down off the roofed sidewalk at the front of the stores.

'And there's been tragedy enough in Providence today, what with that poor Murchison girl lying dead in the funeral parlour,' Roland Decker said.

Steele had started to move away from the law office. He kept watch on the people as they emerged on to the square, but registered only fleeting impressions of them as he made for the mouth of the alley between the livery stable and the boarding house. Harry Krim was a red-headed forty-year-old, broad-shouldered and pot-bellied, dressed in a shirt and leather waist apron. Decker was pushing sixty and had a round head that was almost bald. His neck was short and his build was stocky. He wore a suit. The couple from the stage depot could be mother and son. The four men and two women who had come out of the stores were all past fifty. Everyone was still shocked by the sights and sounds of the break out from the town lock-up. Only Krim showed overt interest in the impassive-faced Virginian who angled across the square in a gait that was grimly determined, and at length demanded to know:

'What do you figure you're doin', stranger?'

Steele halted, turned from the waist and directed a cold-eyed, unblinking gaze at the man who stood outside the entrance of his saloon. Answered evenly: 'I reckon I could be asking to get myself into the same place as Chrissy Murchison, feller.' His eyes moved along their sockets, to look away from the glowering Krim and the suddenly nervous Decker and at the other Providence citizens on the square. Most of them had come to a halt in their progress toward where Miss Attwood continued to stand at the law office entrance. He challenged: 'But that'll mean one of you will have to kill me?'

A tense silence of several stretched seconds followed this. And few people were able to meet and hold Steele's steady, somehow arrogantly curious gaze. Most elected to look quickly away from him and glower their anger at Krim.

'We're no killers!' the saloon-keeper snarled, and was abruptly as discomfited as his fellow citizens.

'Do whatever you feel you must, Mr Steele!' the schoolteacher invited curtly, and Krim was relieved to have the pressure of attention diverted from him. Then, her tone hardened to imply a threat that seemed to carry far more weight than the one the red-headed man had started to make. 'Just so long as it harms nobody?'

Steele acknowledged this with an almost imperceptible nod of his head, then continued toward the alley: aware of many pairs of eyes trained upon his back. But if any of the stares were hostile, the effect was more than counter-balanced by the general feeling of apprehension as, once more, the people converged on the law office. More than those who had been in the buildings on the square now. For some others were coming along the street to the south, their nervous curiosity aroused by the shooting and shouting in their usually quiet town.

Blanche Knight, who was in her fifties and grossly overweight, halted at the foot of the steps from the porch of her boarding house. And accused: 'You're some kinda man, mister. Pickin' on a defenceless woman of advanced years. Yes indeed, some kinda man!'

Her fleshy face was set with a scowl that hardened by the moment, in the same manner as her tone became harder. And for a moment Steele felt an urge to a new anger as he hesitated at the mouth of the alley, the right side of which was flanked by the Knight house. But he fought against the provocation and had beaten it by the time he turned his head to look at the woman who stood no more than five feet tall and probably weighed a hundred and seventy flabby pounds. Was able to show her a neutral expression and to match it with his tone as he responded:

'Miss Attwood did the picking by showing up when she did, ma'am.'

'And not so much of the advanced years, Blanche!' the schoolteacher protested indignantly as she came toward the boarding house, while everyone else gathered into a close-packed throng to peer in through the doorway and windows of the law office.

Steele went on down into the shade of the alley, feeling the skin of his face get taut as a frown of anger now demanded a place. But he was able to bite back on the obscenity that was formed by the shape of his lips. He didn't need anybody to tell him he had been wrong to draw a knife against the local schoolteacher. He had known that an instant after he lunged toward Lavinia Attwood with the knife in his gloved hand. When the impulse to mindless rage had started to diminish against the overwhelming odds of reason. But by then he was committed. Needed to sustain the pretence that he was prepared to maim or kill the hapless woman. And since she had told him what he could have discovered by far less dramatic means, the strain of keeping a tight rein on his emotions had steadily increased. Anger with himself, with Clay Murchison, with Billy Baxter, with Sheriff Fallows, with the whole damn town: with the whole damn world!

You don't know how close you came to getting yourself killed, you ugly fat bitch, Steele thought as he rounded the corner at the rear of Harlan Grout's livery stable. And thudded a tight-clenched fist into an open palm.

'Please, mister, I didn't mean to——'

Steele saw Arlene Forrester emerge from the trees beyond where his wagon was parked between the back of the stable and a corral in which two heavy horses were grazing. She came to a standstill and her fleshy face expressed shock.

'Arlene?' he asked, perplexed.

'I just come this way to get to the meetin' hall, mister,' the black woman blurted. 'It's the shortest way from my place. It's the afternoon when I always clean up in the meetin' hall. I didn't fix to creep up on you nor nothin' like that.'

Her initial fear gradually reduced, and now she peered inquisitively at the Virginian. Who suddenly realised he had not simply thought about his feeling toward Blanche Knight. He must have spoken aloud, and Arlene Forrester had thought he was talking to her. And his frown of confusion had started to ease the black woman's anxiety before he told her:

'Not you, Arlene.'

She sighed away the last remnants of uneasiness and started toward the wagon, smiling broadly as she said: 'I'm real glad about that, mister. Real glad they turned you loose from the lock-up, too.'

Steele made no response as he climbed up into the wagon and first retrieved the Colt Hartford rifle. Immediately felt utterly calm. So there were not even any dregs of tension to be drained out of him when he slid a section of the hope chest's false bottom aside. And saw the sheaves of bills and the gunnysack of gold nuggets were still safe in the secret compartment.

'Want to thank you again for taking care of the wagon and team for me, Arlene,' he told her after he had climbed down.

She had paused at the rear end of the alley between the livery and the bank. Replied with a shake of her head: 'It was little enough, mister. After you took care of buryin' Rosebud and then brought the child here.'

'Where's he now?' Steele asked with just scant interest

as he made to retrace his footsteps to the front of the livery, for the big double doors at the rear were padlocked.

'Mrs Marlow said she'd tend Zachery for while I'm doin' my chores. For a day or so, anyway. Until I can figure things out about the child. I wouldn't have left him at the preacher's house if that half-witted Billy was stayin' there. But he's done gone runnin' off again to his hideyhole. Must've done somethin' bad wrong to——'

'How's that, Arlene?' Steele cut in sharply, abruptly keenly interested in what the black woman was saying as he came to a halt.

'I wouldn't have left a baby in a house with that crazy——'

'I've got that part,' the Virginian interrupted the woman again. 'You say there's a place Baxter runs to when he's done something wrong?'

'Sure is, mister. The old Sanderson place out along Timber Creek. That's where the sheriff had to go bring him back from the time after the trouble with Randell girl. Since that time it's where Billy always runs to whenever folks say he's done somethin' real bad. And most times he ain't done it anyways.'

Despite her mistrust of the mentally retarded man, Arlene Forrester obviously felt a degree of sympathy for him: probably born of an affinity because she had to endure a share of the prejudice that existed in Providence.

'Where's Timber Creek, Arlene?' Steele asked as the black woman shook her head sadly and frowned at memories of past injustices against Baxter.

She gestured with a hand and answered absently: 'It cuts off of the Providence River out to the north-aways, mister. I was at the preacher's house, doin' my cleanin' chores there, when Billy comes chasin' home. Sweatin' and blubbin' like Satan hisself is after him. Don't reckon he heard what I says to him. Nor the preacher nor Mrs

Marlow. Just chases into his room and straight out again. Off he goes back outta the stable. We just knows he must've been accused of doin' somethin' real bad wrong, mister. But it turned out real well for me. Mrs Marlow, she says she'd just love to tend to Zachery for awhile. So with that crazy man gone off to the Sanderson place, I feels safe to leave him there. Otherwise, I'd have had to bring him with me to the meetin' hall like I took him to the preacher's house and——'

'I'm grateful to you,' Steele broke in on the woman whose tone had become preoccupied again, her mind obviously concerned with the well-being of Zachery Petrie.

'Like I already told you, mister, it ain't nothin' to what——'

She broke off of her own volition now, as she saw that Steele had moved out of sight and maybe earshot into the alley on one side of the livery. Then she shrugged and went into the alley on the opposite side. The Virginian had a head start, and also moved faster. He had the double doors of the livery open and was inside by the time the black woman reached the square, which was deserted again. For everyone had withdrawn after the scene of the gaolbreak had been vicariously examined—like the citizens of Providence felt they might be considered guilty by association if they were seen to spend too long within the vicinity of the law office. Thus was Arlene Forrester a lonely figure as she and her truncated, early afternoon shadow moved across an acute angle at the corner of the brilliantly bright, blisteringly hot square. Probably still reflecting anxiously upon her responsibility for the orphan child of her dead niece: and so not susceptible to an awareness of being watched from shadowed windows and doorways. But she was studied solely as something moving that caught the eye in the hot, silent, stillness.

Then, after she had entered the meeting hall, Adam Steele emerged from the livery stable, his rifle still sloped

134

to a shoulder as he led his own grey gelding and Clay Murchison's strawberry roan horse on improvised rope lead lines. The Virginian, too, was partially detached from his immediate surroundings, but his thoughts about what he might learn at the old Sanderson place out along Timber Creek were not so persuasive that he failed to be conscious of the watchers in the stores and the saloon and the stage line depot. Watchers who surveyed him with apprehension or malevolence, resenting him for his part in shattering the undemanding peace of their town.

But nobody watched him from the boarding house. Until he was at the back of the alley and a door in the rear of the Knight place was cracked open. And Lavinia Attwood announced:

'I overheard what was said between Arlene Forrester and you, Mr Steele.'

He came to a standstill and the horses waited patiently as he looked inquiringly at the schoolteacher to answer: 'Wasn't anything either of us should be ashamed of, as I recall, lady?'

Then he moved the horses to the wagon and turned them to position them for harnessing. While he did this he could hear the rasping voices of a disagreement between the schoolteacher and the boarding house keeper just inside the threshold of the building. Before Blanche Knight warned with shrill-voiced irritability:

'Very well, Lavinia, on your own head be it!'

The door was slammed closed and Steele looked across to see that Miss Attwood was left on the outside. She said, with a thin veneer of dignity smoothing her agitation: 'I would deem it a great favour if you will allow me to accompany you, Mr Steele?'

'And why would you want to do that?' Steele asked.

'The Sanderson property is not easy to locate. I will be able to direct you right to it.'

'And . . ?'

135

She pulled a face, chiding herself, then sighed and confirmed: 'My motives are not entirely unselfish. I would ask that you allow me to talk with Billy Baxter before you approach him. When he is as disturbed as he is today, he is liable to respond with violence if he is not treated carefully. And I would like to think that my charge upon you that you cause no harm to any citizen of Providence was well taken, Mr Steele?'

Steele had continued with the task of putting the two horses in the traces, and did not pause when he answered: 'All right, Miss Attwood. We have a deal.'

She was fleetingly surprised at how readily he agreed to what she wanted of him. Then felt the need to augment: 'It could be for your own benefit, too, Mr Steele. Over and above me acting as your guide, I mean. Billy is just as likely to pre-empt an attack by you. If he feels you had a hand in causing this new trouble for him. I'm sure you are most capable of taking care of your——'

'Yes, Miss Attwood,' the Virginian broke in. 'But only for most of the time. You want to get aboard the wagon now? I'm about ready to leave.'

She had difficulty in climbing up by way of the wheel in the long, black dress. But managed it in the end by accepting a hand from Steele, who had got up on to the seat from the other side of the wagon. Then the rear door of the boarding house opened and Blanche Knight accused:

'You're actin' like a fool, Lavinia! You'll be sorry! No good will come of this! You mark my words!'

The door was crashed angrily back into the frame a second time as Steele let off the brakes and ordered with reins and a curt word of command that the team should move off and make a left turn into the alley between the livery stable and the bank.

'Blanche could well be correct,' Miss Attwood allowed with a sigh. 'Perhaps I am a fool? But schoolteachers are not blessed with any God-given right to be smart all the time.'

'If you're having second thoughts, I can let you off, lady,' the Virginian told her evenly.

'No. No thank you, Mr Steele. I promised to act as your guide. And I owe it to Billy Baxter to do what I can to see he comes to no harm.' She looked hard into his profile, and when she saw that he was not going to alter the set of his impassive expression, she injected a plea into her voice to ask: 'I may rely upon co-operation, Mr Steele?'

'I can't promise to handle him with kid gloves, Miss Attwood,' the Virginian told her flatly, heard her catch her breath, and then turned to show her an almost warm smile as he held up his hands holding the reins. Added: 'I wear the buckskin kind.'

12

As they emerged from the mouth of the alley and drove across the corner of the square to get to the start of the trail north, both the driver and passenger could not fail to know they were being surreptitiously watched with shocked, keen interest. And it was probable that the clop of hooves and the rattle of wheelrims masked a buzz of intrigued talk about Lavinia Attwood's presence aboard the hay wagon laden with household chattels driven by an escaped prisoner.

'You'll have to forgive me for not enjoying your humour, Mr Steele,' the woman said, peering directly ahead so that she was not tempted to look toward any of the points from which she was being watched and discussed by her fellow citizens. 'You are obviously more experienced than I at rising above the tragedies of life.'

Her blue eyes were as bright as her features were sharp for most of the time. But until she had run the gamut of curiosity they were dull and her face looked worn and wearied. Then, on the trail beyond the northern town limits marker that was fixed to the rear wall of the meeting hall, the high tension that had so dramatically aged the woman drained out of her on a sigh.

'Had more than my fair share, I reckon,' Steele said flatly.

'I'm sure,' she replied absently, and required a few more seconds to recover her composure. Instructed: 'You keep along this trail until it runs beside the Providence River. About a half mile. Then a spur goes off to the north west where a tributory joins the river. The spur fords the river and we take that.'

'Got you, Miss Attwood,' Steele said, and was easily able to resist an impulse to remind her that Arlene Forrester had told him as much: with the implication that he didn't think the old Sanderson place was going to be difficult for him to find. Instead, he asked: 'Will you tell me what happened at the Providence bank this morning?'

'You don't know?' She was surprised both by the abrupt manner of the question and his ignorance.

'Your sheriff was in a hurry to hit the trail, Miss Attwood. Didn't take the time to do anything more than lock up Murchison and me.'

She sighed once more and shook her head as she said: 'I fear Leonard Fallows is somewhat out of his depth in dealing with such a serious matter as this.'

'I may have a score to settle with him because he tossed me into a cell without good reason, lady,' Steele said, his tone and expression suddenly hard. 'But that will only be if I have any hate to spare after I've got better than even with Parker and his two partners.'

His abrupt change of attitude provoked a gasp from the elderly woman, who had thought she was in total control of herself again. 'Parker? I'm afraid I don't know of anyone——'

'Parker, Tait and Ashton robbed the town bank this morning. I think. And killed Clay Murchison's wife, I've been told. I think a lot and I've been told a little. What I know for fact isn't very much at all. But it's enough to give me good reason to kill Parker, Tait, and Ashton. We've got time to kill getting to the old Sanderson place.

139

I reckoned I might learn something. After all, you are a teacher, Miss Attwood.'

The smile he showed her this time was even less warm than before as he managed to confine the futile impulse to anger into the ice cold ball at the pit of his stomach.

'My, Mr Steele,' the grey-haired, black-garbed woman on the seat beside him murmured. 'What on earth did those three men do to you to inspire such high feelings of enmity toward them?'

'Steered me back on to the killing trail.'

Her bright blue eyes directed a penetrating stare at him, but once again the impassive set of his faintly sweat-sheened, slightly bristled face signalled he was not about to elaborate on the cryptic comment. And she faced the front again to say:

'I only know from first hand that I was awakened at dawn by the most awesome scream I have ever heard, Mr Steele. My room at the boarding house is at the front and I can see right across the square from the window. I reached the window in time to see three riders race their horses on to the start of this trail. They could have started from the stage depot, the bank or the livery stable. From my window on the same side of the square, I was not able to see. But then Mr Kenway, who lives in the back of his hardware store across the square, saw the door of Ethan Brady's bank was open and shouted that it looked as if the bank had been robbed.

'I hurried to dress and went downstairs and out on to the porch with Blanche. But Tom Knight was already at the bank. With Mr Kenway and Harold Archer from the grocery store. While Tom Knight was being physically sick to his stomach at the bank doorway, Mr Kenway and Harold Archer ordered all the women to stay back. Then Mr Kenway went to bring the sheriff.'

She looked at Steele again as she said with an almost apologetic tone: 'From this point it will be hearsay?'

140

'You were closer to what happened than me, Miss Attwood,' Steele told her. 'And you know the people you talked with better than I do.'

The schoolteacher peered along the tree-flanked trail, and the Virginian knew she was tensing herself to talk of events that revolted her.

'Ethan Brady was awakened at his house by a loud banging on the door. It was Mrs Murchison. She was badly beaten. Her face was bruised and bleeding and she could not stand straight from being punched in the stomach. She told Ethan Brady her husband had attacked her in a drunken rage and she was leaving him. But she was determined to have a share of his money that was lodged in the bank safe. Clay Murchison was known to mistreat his wife, Mr Steele——'

'Yes, lady, I know,' Steele interrupted, to prevent Lavinia Attwood from launching into a lengthy explanation for the banker's motives in giving a woman access to her husband's savings. 'I spent a little time with Chrissy Murchison. And for awhile her husband was in a mood to talk about his marriage.'

'Quite so,' the woman countered and hurried on with the hearsay account, like she was eager to have done with it. 'Ethan Brady went with Mrs Murchison to his bank and opened up for her. But as soon as he unlocked the safe, the three men came into the building. They bound and gagged Ethan and when Mrs Murchison tried to apologise to him one of the men knocked her senseless. Ethan could only gather that she was not a willing party to the robbery. They cleared the safe of all the cash money and some jewellery, but they were not prepared to let it be at that. One of them took out a knife. And in front of Ethan Brady they tore the clothes off Mrs Murchison. And just as she began to recover consciousness, they . . . they cut her. Cut her . . .'

'Cut out her sex, Miss Attwood?' Steele supplied to

relieve the elderly spinster of the need to search for an appropriate term.

'Yes. Yes, that's right.' The horror that the image of the brutal act had stirred within her was briefly displaced by gratitude toward the Virginian. Then she was struck by a doubt and asked quickly: 'I thought you didn't know what happened at the bank?'

'The same three men did the same thing to Rosebud Petrie,' he answered and she raised both hands to her mouth, as if to block something with more substance than a gasp from escaping her throat. 'Which landed me with a baby,' Steele went on as he heard the rippling of running water not far ahead. 'Which got me involved with the Murchisons. Which almost got me killed. Got me beaten up though. Then got me locked up in a hick town gaol by a lawman who's out of his depth. Like I told you, Miss Attwood, I'll maybe let Len Fallows off the hook. Long as I can get to Parker and his two buddies.'

'I can see you have been put to considerable inconvenience because of their sadistic——'

'It was Chrissy Murchison who caused me to be beaten up,' Steele said as the Providence River and the trail closed with each other in a wide clearing. 'If she hadn't done that, they'd have killed me. I'm too late to save *her* life.'

The woman raised a hand, intending to point to where the spur trail cut off to the left and forded the hundred-feet wide river, that flowed faster here than at either end of the ravine to the south of the town. But Steele was already steering the team into a gentle turn. And the schoolteacher remained silent until the water had ceased to splash and the wagon rode relatively smoothly again, after running clear of the pebble-strewn riverbed. Then she said:

'She died almost at once, according to Ethan. From shock as much as the physical wound, Doctor Mackay thinks. That is why the end was so mercifully quick. The poor creature would have died in any event. She was weakened, too, by the earlier ill-treatment she received. Her body and limbs were black and blue, I heard it said.'

'Clay Murchison hit her just once in the face last night,' Steele said. 'The rest of the lumps must have been given her by Parker or Tait or Ashton.'

'I'm sure the sheriff will accept that when he has time and opportunity to consider the situation. But after seeing the corpse and hearing Ethan Brady's account . . . Well, Mr Steele, is it any wonder that he and the men he deputised were unwilling to be distracted from setting off to hunt down those monsters?'

'I do more than wonder about it lady. But I'm biased.'

'Quite so.'

A lengthy pause followed this, as the spur trail followed a meandering course set by the creek to the right. The going was harder than on the main trail, for they were on a steady upgrade and the spur was not smoothed by frequent use. It was rutted and weed-choked and littered with fallen branches from the high firs that grew close to the side of the spur on the left, and to the far bank of the fast-running Timber Creek on the right. Steele concentrated his attention on what lay ahead, for on all other sides an army of men with hatred in their hearts for him could have been hidden. So he elected to trust that his sixth sense for lurking danger would alert him to a potential attack. From a force lesser in number than an army. A lone man, a trio of them, or a seven-strong posse.

'I understand your motives for seeking out the men to kill them, Mr Steele,' the schoolteacher said at length. 'But why do you think Billy Baxter can help you?'

'I'm guessing, lady. Baxter saw a wanted poster for Parker and his partners in the law office. It was that sent him bolting home to the Marlow house. Then out here maybe.'

'Billy Baxter cannot read, Mr Steele,' Lavinia Attwood said, perplexed.

'I guessed that. But I reckon he knows a wanted poster when he sees one. And the one issued on Parker, Tait and Ashton carries pretty good drawings of them.'

'I see! You think he recognised the men? But why should he——'

'Like I said, I'm guessing,' Steele reminded her. 'Something made Baxter bolt out of the law office even though Murchison held a gun on him. And sent him running to his room in the preacher's stable. To get to Murchison's other gun, maybe. That something was one of a dozen or so wanted posters he saw in the sheriff's desk drawer, Miss Attwood. And I'm not prepared to stretch coincidence beyond more than three wanted men being around a small town like Providence at any one time.'

'Yes, quite so,' the woman agreed thoughtfully. 'But why should Billy . . ?' She shook her head and made a sound of self-deprecation. 'Of course, you are theorising. And while Len Fallows with the posse and Mr Murchison on his own account are endeavouring to track down the murderers by their own means, it is worth attempting a short cut?'

'You've got it. Now do you mind answering a question for me, Mrs Attwood?'

'If I'm able, Mr Steele.' And for the first time since they set out from in back of Harlan Grout's livery stable, she acknowledged the presence of sweat on her face: produced a lacy handkerchief from inside a sleeve of the black dress, and delicately patted at the salty sheen of moisture on her brow and cheeks. The white satin and lace trimming was stained with powder as well as dampness when she replaced the handkerchief.

'Why are you so worried about what happens to Baxter? What is he to you?'

She nodded to let him know she was aware of his glance

144

at her. Then replied: 'I heard Arlene Forrester tell you how Len Fallows had to come out here to get Billy Baxter after the trouble involving Gertrude Randell. I had a hand in that, Mr Steele. It's almost five years ago now. Trudy Randell was ten or eleven at the time. A student at the school. She was late several mornings running and when she eventually ran out of the usual excuses she said all the earlier ones were lies. Billy was stopping her each morning and giving her a penny to . . . to look at her and touch her.' She vented a deep sigh and shook her head. 'I accepted the girl's word and informed the sheriff. The news of what was afoot spread fast, and Len Fallows was at the head of a virtual lynch mob when he reached the Marlow house. Fortunately, Billy had heard he was in trouble and he ran away. Everyone knew where he would be. It was the Sandersons who had taken care of him and brought him out here to California when he was a child.

'By the time the sheriff was ready to come out here for Billy, the mob consisted of almost every able-bodied adult in Providence. It really did seem that Billy had no chance of surviving that day, Mr Steele. The fact that he is mentally deficient . . . Well, I'm certain feelings would not have run so high against a normal man.'

They had reached the crest of the long grade across which the creek and the trail wound. And started out over a plateau that was as thickly wooded here as on the slope. The creek flowed with less noisy urgency, and birds could be heard in the mixed timber at either side of the trail and water course that inscribed a gentle arc from the west toward the north.

'But perhaps it was his dim-wittedness that saved him from being lynched,' Lavinia Attwood went on. 'Trudy Randell was with us. Her mother and father had insisted she come here to confront Billy. But something about him when he was found; something about the way he cowered in front of Len Fallows and pleaded he knew nothing about the girl must have touched her heart. But whatever the reason, she shouted a retraction. She was late for school because she hated lessons and dawdled. The money she said Billy gave her she had stolen from her parents' savings jar.

'That is why I feel responsible for Billy, Mr Steele. Oh, I'm sure everyone believed the girl lied in the first instance. But mud sticks. The Randells moved away from Providence shortly afterwards, but Billy has always been looked upon with more distrust than ever since it all happened. And I'm sure I could have prevented that if only I had questioned Trudy Randell more thoroughly. Instead of being as ready as everyone else to jump to the conclusion that she had told the truth. Primarily because Billy Baxter is the way he is. I feel a man such as you will understand that, Mr Steele?'

'Reckon so, Mrs Attwood,' he confirmed.

'And you'll allow me to talk with Billy should he be out here and prepared to commit violence because he thinks he's——'

'On one condition,' Steele cut in.

'You didn't stipulate conditions when we set out!'

'That you don't lie to me anymore.'

'Lie?'

He gestured toward a leaning post to the right of the trail, immediately opposite another post that still stood five feet straight up. Rusted pivot pins in the side of the standing post showed where a gate had once hung many years ago. Burnt with branding irons into the askew gatepost was the still clearly legible lettering that spelled out vertically the name SANDERSON. He told her without rancour:

'There are times when I act as dimwitted as Baxter is, Miss Attwood. But I don't reckon I'd have had any trouble following Arlene Forrester's directions to get here.'

She frowned and said, a little huskily: 'A white lie, I'll admit. But in certain instances the end must justify the means? As I'm certain a man like you will agree?'

Before he was to reply, the Virginian's attention was drawn elsewhere. And he reined the team to a halt. Heard the woman's short gasp of mild surprise to his right as he scanned the timber that crowded close to the trail on the left.

'Is something——'

The schoolteacher's surprise had begun to expand toward anxiety. Now her throat constricted with fear to curtail her voice. This as a figure appeared from among the trees. Showing himself at the point where Steele had sensed a hidden watcher.

'Easy,' Steele told the startled woman, and abandoned his own move to reach into the rear of the wagon for the Colt Hartford. This as they both recognised the acned face and coverall-garbed frame of Billy Baxter. Who advanced on the stalled wagon with a slow, careful gait: the second of Clay Murchison's Remington revolvers clutched tightly in his right hand that was thrust out at arm's length. The gun hand trembled a little, wavering the muzzle of the revolver. But the aim never shifted far from Steele's chest.

'It's okay, Miss Attwood,' Billy said in a strained voice, blinking beads of sweat off his eyelashes and licking his lips. 'I got him covered real well, so you ain't got nothin' to worry about no more.'

'But Billy, I'm not——'

'It's worked out real well, ain't it?' the man with a child's mind pressed on. Gaining in confidence by the moment as he steadied his aim with a two-handed grip and peered fixedly at the Virginian. Seemed not to hear the woman's attempt to correct his mistaken impression that she was here against her will.

'How's that?' Steele asked, and shot a sidelong glance

at Lavinia Attwood that expressed a tacit demand she remain silent.

'I done wrong to make it so you and Mr Murchison could get outta the lock-up. It was a bad thing I done. But now it's all right. That Mr Murchison, he's gonna get what he deserves, seems to me. And I got you covered so you can be put back in the lock-up. But if you try to get away, mister, I'll shoot you. Won't bother me none to shoot you. Way you made Miss Attwood come with you. Miss Attwood's always been real good to me. Especially since the time when they figured I'd done somethin' bad and I didn't do it. Not at all.'

Steele heard the woman take in a breath as a sign she intended to speak again. But he spoke first.

'Where's Mr Murchison getting what he deserves, Billy?'

Baxter gestured with his head along the trail. 'At the Sanderson place. He came by me, ridin' what looked like Mr Decker's horse. I hid when I heard a horse comin'. And I didn't see who it was until he was by where I was hid. He was too far off to shoot then. And I wouldn't mind shootin' him none. Way he beat up on that wife of his so much. She was always good to me, that Mrs Murchison. A real kind lady. But it don't matter none. Them men at the Sanderson place got him. I crept up to there and saw. Come back to here when I heard this wagon comin'.'

'Men, Billy?' the woman asked. 'You mean Sheriff Fallows and——'

'Mr Fallows?' Baxter's sub-normal mind was confused by the mention of a name that did not figure in this part of his tale.

'Or maybe the men in the picture you saw in the sheriff's office?' Steele suggested.

The acne-ravaged face spread with a smile and he nodded his head eagerly. 'Hey, yeah! Them three. I seen them at the Sanderson place when I come out this mornin'. Come to figure if I should let you outta the lock-up. You and Mr Murchison. Dollar sounded real good, but I knew it was wrong. Always come out to the Sanderson place when I have to think things through. But I seen three men at the place. And I didn't like the look of them, I can tell you. Made up my mind to let you and Mr Murchison outta the lock-up. Figured out how. With the gun on the tray with the grub. Then I seen the wanted poster. Couldn't read the letterin' on it, but I knew who them men was. Know what a wanted poster is. Figured that if I come out to the Sanderson place and make them prisoners, Mr Fallows nor nobody else'd think so bad of me for gettin' the gun to you and Mr Murchison.'

The smile had gradually faded from his face. And the Remington began to waver in its aim again, despite the double-handed grip. This as, seemingly, Billy Baxter's confidence in his plan diminished with the telling of it.

'Billy, please put the gun away before you truly do something bad,' Lavinia Attwood advised, her tone gently placating. 'I came here with Mr Steele of my own free will because I——'

Her voice trailed away just as she began to get her meaning through to the confused man on the ground. And she, Baxter and Steele all listened intently to the sound that had caused her to pause. A regular thudding, of metal on metal. Coming from further along the trail. It lasted for just a few seconds and the woman rasped to end the short silence:

'What was that?'

Steele completed his turn on the seat and brought the Colt Hartford out of the back as he answered: 'Somebody using a hammer, I reckon.'

'Hey, mister!' Baxter blurted. And thrust the Remington further forward, fear contorting his blotched and pitted features as he realised what the Virginian was doing.

The metal striking metal sound began to ring out again

and Steele growled as he cocked his rifle in full view of the terrified man on the ground: 'Something you overlooked, Billy.'

Baxter gagged like he was about to be sick to his stomach.

The hammering ended once more.

A shrill scream cut suddenly through the hot, pine-scented air of mid-afternoon.

Baxter gave a strangled cry, whirled and bolted back into the timber from where he had emerged.

Lavinia Attwood rasped again, with a greater depth of feeling: 'What was that?'

Steele reached into the back of the wagon to bring out Murchison's Winchester and swung to the ground before he drawled: 'A sound reason for you to stay here, lady.'

13

The Virginian leaned his own rifle against the wagon wheel and looked up at the horrified woman to rasp: 'Can you shoot a Winchester?'

She had to swallow hard before she found her voice to answer with a vigorous shake of her head: 'No! No, I've never had occasion to fire any kind of gun.'

'Maybe now you do,' he told her. 'Watch.' He twice pumped the lever action of the repeater to eject unfired shells from the top of the frame. Then instructed as he stooped to retrieve the live shells: 'You have to aim it and squeeze the trigger between doing that. Got it, lady?'

She gulped again and this time failed to release what was needed to speak an affirmative. But she nodded and continued to stare with awed fascination at the Winchester as Steele pressed the two shells back into the magazine through the loading gate.

'Forget the reloading, Miss Attwood,' he said with less urgency as he beckoned for her to get down from the wagon. 'Maybe it won't even be necessary to fire one shot. Best you get off the wagon and hide. Underneath or in the timber.'

'Oh, my,' she gasped as she accepted his help to reach the ground, and took hold of the rifle.

'And, Miss Attwood?'

'Yes?' She vented a small gasp as she accepted the full weight of the Winchester and was surprised by how heavy it was.

'See who you aim at before you fire. You don't want to hurt Billy Baxter. Nor me neither, I hope.'

There was noisy movement in her throat, but the Virginian had turned away from her and powered into a run along the trail before she had finished taking the breath for a response that would have been more lengthy than a few monosyllables. And Lavinia Attwood was immediately banished from his mind as he devoted his full attention to watching for a sign of Billy Baxter: aware that in the confused, underdeveloped mind of the man he could still be registered as an enemy. For the sudden burst of activity that followed the scream might well have acted to wipe from Baxter's mind everything that had been said since he showed himself at the wagon.

Then the Virginian was close enough to the source of the earlier hammering and the scream to hear a low, throaty whimpering sound. An expression of pain such as a dog might make as it licked its wounds after a beating, while in his mind is more than a slight suspicion that this is merely a respite before the infliction of further punishment. But it was not a dog that was whimpering. It was Clay Murchison. And he was in no position to lick his wounds. For he was trapped in a high-backed rocking chair. His ankles and feet were tied with rope to the front legs and the forward extensions of the curved runners and another length of rope had been wound around his torso and the chair back several times, from his midriff to his neck. There were no rope bonds to hold his arms along the arms of the chair. Instead, a nail had been driven through the back of each of his splayed hands and into the wood beneath his palms. A final blow with the hammer at each side had bent over the heads of the nails to prevent the suffering man trying to wrench his tortured hands free.

'How are you feelin', old feller?' the scar-faced Lonnie Ashton asked with mock pity.

'We tried to make you as comfortable as we could, Mr Murchison,' Denny Parker added in much the same tone. He held up a liquor bottle. 'Seein' as how you did us the favour of bringin' us out some fine whiskey.'

He tilted the bottle to his lips as Stan Tait rasped through his prominent teeth displayed in a sadistic grin:

'Thought you'd better be sittin' down. On account of the shock might make you keel over. Old guy like you are.'

Steele watched the scene and listened to the talking and the whimpering from some five hundred feet distance. Concealed in a clump of brush between the end of the trail and the creek. From the side of the thicket the water course started a gentle curve across an area of weed-choked ground that looked as if it had once been culti-vated. Then ran behind a small timber and fieldstone, single-story house. And, beyond this, a taller barn that was built at a right angle to the front of the house to form two adjacent sides of a yard. One of the broken and leaning fences of a large corral formed a third side, opposite the house. The side that was approached by the trail was open, and thus did the Virginian have a clear view of where Clay Murchison was an agonised prisoner in the rocking chair, faced by his brutal captors, just outside the doorway at the centre of the house's façade.

Because the trio of killers with twisted minds were so engrossed in torturing a new victim beneath the dazzlingly bright and blisteringly hot sun, they were in no frame of mind to be on their guard against intruders. And anyway, the Virginian reasoned as he took in the details of the brutal centrepiece of the tableau and its backdrop of an abandoned and dilapidated ranch, why should the men be anxious on that score? They had hit the town bank and killed Chrissy Murchison there at dawn. Now it was gone mid-afternoon and Providence was less than a half hour's fast riding away. Maybe they had even seen the posse ride on by down at where the spur to this place cut off the main trail?

'You bastards!' Clay Murchison forced out through gritted teeth as Steele shortened the focus of his eyes after peering into the distance where fine-looking country rolled away across gentle hills that were either lushly grassed or thickly timbered.

'Hey, we done good by you, like Stan just told you,' Ashton chided. 'Even sat you in the chair and made sure you wouldn't fall out while you was out cold. Wasn't our fault you come outta it just as Stan was——'

'Why?' the man in the rocker cut in, his gaunt face beaded with the sweat of agony. 'Why not just kill me?'

Steele moved out of the thicket of brush and went down off his haunches on to his belly as he entered the expanse of weeds. Had to struggle to keep his mind free of extraneous notions as he snaked through the three-feet high cover that adequately concealed him but would not stop a bullet. The most insistent thought was concerned with how well this place fitted in his plans for a stud ranch. It would need a great deal of work done, of course. The house and barn needed renovating, fences required fixing and this former crop field through which he was crawling would have to be deep-ploughed to rid it of the weeds.

Also, he told himself grimly with a grimace to match his self anger at the thoughts so inappropriate to the moment, the front yard had to be cleaned up. Of three sadistic killers and the helpless man who they intended should be their next victim.

'That ain't our way, Murchison,' Tait said. 'Not when we got the time.'

'Take pleasure in it,' Ashton taunted.

'And it makes sense for a man to make his pleasures

154

last,' Parker added. 'And we surely did that with that fine-lookin' wife you used to have.'

'God, you friggin'——'

'Not the killin' of her,' Ashton broke in on Murchison's agonised voice. 'The bitch died real fast. But we sure made the pleasure of what went before last a real long time.'

'You hear how she died, Murchison?' Tait asked, his tone suddenly ominously harsh.

'Same way Stan always kills women,' Parker said and sounded almost indifferent. 'Or at least, we figure most of them die pretty soon after he's done with them.'

Steele had not been able to see more than a few inches in front of his face since he entered the high weeds, to haul himself along on his elbows while he gripped the rifle in both hands. Then, when he reached the far side of the overgrown field, the side wall of the house blocked his view of most of the front yard. But he could see back to where the trail emerged from the timber. And to one side of this, across from where he had crouched behind the thicket of brush, he spotted Billy Baxter. Over such a distance he could not be totally sure about it, but he thought the blotched and pitted face of the watching man was wreathed with a grin of pleasure at the display of evil he witnessed.

Then the Virginian moved quickly around the corner to the rear of the house: making haste to get out of sight of Baxter in case the man saw him and took it into his sub-normal mind to raise the alarm. If Parker, Tait or Ashton happened to turn from their brutal attentions to Murchison and saw Billy Baxter . . . Well, maybe Steele could make use of such a diversion.

'This is how I do it,' Tait said with a guffaw as Steele reached the doorless doorway in the far end of the rear wall of the house. 'Cut it out of them and dry it. Got started with squaws up in the Dakotas when I was fightin'

Injuns with the army. High payin' market for 'em back east. Since I got started, I found out the white ones bring the top dollar. This one here's what I cut outta your wife.'

The Virginian was inside the one-roomed house now. Picking his way among the whole and broken furniture and the saddles and gear of the men who stood in a short arc before their prisoner just beyond the doorless front doorway.

Clay Murchison vented a shriek of anguish that was longer and louder than that of pain when he had come out of unconsciousness. Reacting to the sight of the chunk of flesh, quite obviously cut from a woman, that the buck-toothed Tait displayed for him. Holding it in the palm of a filthy hand after he had unwrapped it from a piece of rag stained with the blood that had not congealed on the tissue.

'Ain't that somethin'?' Lonnie Ashton yelled excitedly. And exploded with a burst of laughter as he hooked a foot under one of the runners to set the chair rocking. 'Ain't no one else does that! Stan ain't no copycat—more like a pussycat, uh?'

All three of Murchison's torturers were venting gusts of laughter now. Sufficient to totally drown out the low-pitched wailing sound that was the only form of vocal expression of his suffering that the punished man had strength left to force out. And this barrage of guffawing and chortling and giggling also acted to blanket any small noise the Virginian made as he crossed the room, his lean features hard-set as he smelled his own sweat against the stale odours that clung to the derelict house.

There were no inappropriate notions in his mind now. Just a dual image of the two women he knew these sadists had killed. One he had known just fleetingly after her path crossed the bloody one they rode. The other . . .

'Goddamn!' Parker blurted and let fall the bottle as he saw Steele step on to the threshold, six feet in back of where the chair rocked.

Rocked more violently over a longer distance now. Sent into this exaggerated pitching motion by both Parker and Ashton. Who had drawn knives. Thrust them toward positions where the next forward swing of the chair would impale Murchison's eyes upon the glinting tips of the blades. This while the laughing Tait continued to hold his gory trophy like a proud collector displaying his most highly prized trophy.

Parker hurled away his knife.

Steele shot the buck-toothed man first. For no other reason than the hunk of human meat in his hand made him the most hated man at the moment. The bullet took him in the roof of his gaping mouth after it had smashed through his prominent teeth. And he was sent sprawling backwards, arms flung wide to the sides and blood gouting from his suddenly silent mouth.

Before he crashed to the ground amid billows of powder dust, Steele had thumbed back the hammer of the rifle and swung the barrel a fraction to the left. Then squeezed the trigger a second time. To pump a bullet into the chest of Lonnie Ashton. Which stopped the man's heart just as his hand that had released the knife formed a fist around his holstered revolver. He went down with a corkscrewing action, his lifeblood blossoming out over the sweat-stained shirt between his broad suspenders.

A rifle began to explode a barrage of shots. Close by, but not in the immediate vicinity of the sun-bright yard where the chair with its captive occupant slowed the pace of its rocking. Then a revolver began to be fired, less rapidly and with a less obtrusive sound.

Parker made the mistake of glancing toward the gunfire as he got his Colt almost clear of the holster. And saw there was no danger to him from Lavinia Attwood and Billy Baxter. For the schoolteacher on the trail and the mentally retarded man at the fringe of the timber were exploding their weapons at the cloudless sky. But by the time the man with a crooked nose and bags beneath his eyes had returned his gaze to Steele, the Colt Hartford was cocked again and had been swung across the back of the slowing rocking chair to be aimed at him through the drifting gunsmoke of the two previous shots.

'All right, Steele!' he blurted, and thrust the revolver violently back into the holster. Pushed both hands out to the sides. 'You got me!'

Clay Murchison's revolver in the double-handed grip of Billy Baxter was emptied of its six shells. Lavinia Attwood exploded two more shots from the twelve-round magazine of the rifle, and then realised she had served her purpose. Perhaps later Steele might reflect that Denny Parker could have killed him if the diversion had not been so unexpectedly staged.

'I don't want you, feller,' the Virginian forced out, conscious of the tautness of the skin stretched over his facial bone structure.

The chair became still and Clay Murchison interrupted his ragged breathing to croak: 'I do, mister. I want the bastard. Get me outta this chair and loan me your rifle.'

'You ain't the kind, Steele,' Parker challenged and there was even a trace of a smile on his lean, angular face to signal his mounting confidence. 'Not the kind that would gun down a man that's surrendered himself.'

The arms that he had spread to the sides he now began to raise, bending them at the elbows. And with each inch they came up, so his smile broadened. Then he glanced over a shoulder toward Lavinia Attwood and Billy Baxter, who were hurrying toward the yard.

Murchison sought to tear his hands free. And groaned in pain and frustration as more blood spurted and the nails held firm.

'Are you a betting man, feller?' Steele asked, and knew he was speaking to use up time. Time in which the

Providence sheriff and his posse, maybe, might show up to take away the temptation that was so strong.

'I surely am. And I bet pretty soon I'll be on my way back to New Mexico. Where I'll have another chance to break out of——'

'You lose,' the Virginian cut in. And squeezed the trigger of the Colt Hartford. It was another heart shot, which spilled little blood. But dramatically altered the smile to a mask of disbelief on the broken-nosed face of Parker as the man crashed to the ground on his back.

'Thanks,' Clay Murchison rasped, remarkably calm as he sat in the rocker on a sunny afternoon, head bowed and sighing.

Steele leaned the rifle against the doorframe and moved off the threshold to look more closely at the way the man's hands were nailed to the chair arms. Then surveyed the dust-powdered surface of the yard between the chair and the sprawled, blood-run corpses. Ignored the discarded knives that lay there. First draped Tait's gruesome trophy with the stained rag it had been wrapped in. Then picked up the bottle of rye whiskey Parker had hurled away. It was unbroken and had not spilled all its contents. He offered it to Murchison, who nodded and licked his lips. Drank the equivalent of a half dozen shots to empty it without attempting to turn his head away. Expressed his gratitude tacitly this time.

'Best we get the town doctor out here to work on your hands, feller?'

Murchison nodded again as the schoolteacher, with Baxter at her side, slowed the pace of their approach as they drew close to the corpses and the man nailed in the rocking chair.

'You want to get a horse from the barn, Billy?' Steele asked the over-awed, sub-normal man. 'And go bring the doctor to——'

'I don't ride, mister. But I run real fast!' He threw down

the empty Remington, spun on his heels and powered into a sprint. Eager to get clear of the blood-run scene.

The Providence schoolteacher let the Winchester fall to the yard with less violence as she exclaimed with deep shock: 'Mr Steele, I did not think it possible. You killed a man in cold blood! He did not have a chance!'

'Not for the first time, lady,' the Virginian told her as he went to get his rifle, angled it at the sky and half cocked the hammer. Began to extract the spent shellcases. Then, as he did this, his attention was captured by a plank of wood fixed above the doorway of the house. It was lettered, like the gatepost, with branding irons. A little more weather-ravaged and faded by the passing of time, but still readable. For a moment or so he looked away from the sign that gave the house a name. But instead of meeting the shocked, disapproving gaze of Miss Attwood, he scanned the fine country spread out before the house and barn and corral. This as he concluded cryptically: 'Reckon it's gotten to be easier since the first one right at the start.'

Then he looked up again at the name of the house and took a conscious decision to completely rotate the cylinder of the Colt Hartford. So that every chamber was emptied as his weary eyes studied the sign that read . . .

TRAIL'S END.*

_____

* But will Adam Steele be able to live here in peace at the end of the sunset ride?